WHAT READERS ARE SAYING about *at the Intersection of Blood & Money* . . .

"All I can say is I hope Faith Wood never stops writing! I'm now through all of her books, and this is my favorite!"

—CARMEN NOBLE

"Talk about a cozy mystery! I started reading in bed about 9 one night, picked it up again in the morning, and finished by evening. Now, that's a good read!"

—MARG BELLMAN

"I wait for Wood's books to hit the market—I know I'm in for a good read, and at the Intersection of Blood & Money was exactly what I expected from this author—fantastic!"

—M. DENEFIELD

"Who says a guy can't like a cozy mystery? I've read all of Wood's books, and at the Intersection of Blood & Money ranks in my top two. But, it was hard to choose—all of Wood's books are great!"

—T. BANKMAN

"You know how some writers become predictable? Not Wood. Her characters remain fresh, and she's not afraid to throw in the unexpected—loved at the Intersection of Blood & Money!"

—RANDI CARTMAN

at the

INTERSECTION

of

BLOOD & MONEY

at the

INTERSECTION

of

BLOOD & MONEY

FAITH WOOD

Wood Media
British Columbia, Canada

DEDICATION

To readers who love mystery and intrigue . . .

CHAPTER

1

*N*o matter how many times she left the country, packing didn't get easier—and, it was a pain in the ass. Never knowing how long she would be away from home, it seemed prudent to pack to the max— but, there was always something to forget. "I think that's it," she muttered to herself, surveying her luggage. "It damned well better be . . ."

Colbie sat on the side of her bed, scanning the room for something she forgot, then turned her attention to three yellow legal tablets. Crammed to the gills with information, her notes represented only the outer edge of what she needed to know—it was what lay beneath the obvious that was of ultimate interest. *When it comes down to it,* she thought as she flipped through the tablets' pages, *I don't have crap . . .*

"You ready?" Ryan peered around the door to her bedroom with an alarmed glance. "All of this?"

Momentarily startled, she slid the legal pads into her messenger bag. "What do you mean? I scaled back!"

He knew better than to argue, figuring doing so wouldn't get him anywhere. Besides, they were already late, and making her flight would take some doing. One by one, he lugged baggage to the waiting cab, Kevin taking charge of packing its trunk. "I think we need two cabs," he commented, grunting as he hoisted Colbie's last piece of luggage, stuffing it wherever it would fit. He glanced at the trunk with little usable space remaining. "Where are you going to put your stuff?"

"I'm taking the later flight, thank God . . ."

Kevin grinned at him, catching Colbie walking down the flat's steps from the corner of his eye. "Lucky you . . ."

Minutes later, the cab pulled away from the curb then jockeyed for position in barely moving traffic, its destination predetermined. When booking reservations, Kevin made certain to insist on the company's best driver—although Colbie was usually patient, he learned quickly when she felt rushed, understanding sometimes nosedived.

As traffic crawled, Colbie's thoughts turned to her new case. *Just who is Basile Duchon,* she wondered as she stared out the window. When she returned his call—and, from the moment he answered—he insisted on discussing the matter in person, rather than on the phone. Reluctantly, she agreed, but doing so gave her little to go on for beginning research. When they clicked off, the upshot of the ten-minute conversation amounted to nothing but fluff. Even so, her gut told her to take the case, especially since Ryan presented it to her a few weeks prior.

According to final instructions from her client, upon her arrival, she was to wait at the gate if her contact were, for some unacceptable reason, detained. Under no circumstances was she to strike off on her own, only to contact him later. Of course, Colbie was well versed when it came to his reputation, so she regarded his eccentricities of little importance. She dealt with worse over the years—besides, it added a little more intrigue.

Basile Duchon reached middle age with little to show for his efforts. An early design career landed him squarely on the bottom rung, and it wasn't until shortly after the turn of the twentieth century did his creative aspirations hit their mark. Although many viewed his avant garde flair inappropriate for anything but the red carpet, he proved them wrong when buyers wouldn't leave him alone to design. Create. To change the fashion world for years to come. Those were his true aspirations and, shortly after critics took notice, he fled underground with enough money to hire the best to handle all of his affairs. So, when he called Colbie in person?

Big. Really big.

His English was excellent, although, had it been otherwise, it posed no issue—fluent in French from summers spent in Canada, Colbie was confident in her ability to carry on more than casual conversation. During their phone conversation, there was little question of his superlative education, and she found herself sitting up a little straighter, straining to make certain she understood every word. The bottom line was she was about to enter the fashion world— something completely different. While she was familiar with famous designer names, she knew nothing of the industry— an industry fraught with flamboyant façade and conscious corruption.

Ryan slapped Kevin with new details of the case before climbing into his cab. "Make sure," he directed, "you deep dive into Duchon's background. Find out what you can— what I gave you will get you started, but, I'm warning you— there isn't much. When this guy goes underground . . ."

Kevin nodded. "I get it. Anything else?"

"After I meet Colbie in Paris, she's going to want to get started on the investigation immediately—Fashion Week is in six weeks, and we don't want to miss a thing. Research who will be attending, if possible, and send us the results as soon as you know them . . ."

"I'm sorry I asked!"

Ryan laughed, got in and closed the door, then opened the window a crack. "Have fun!

Colbie considered the quick flight from Geneva to Paris a good thing, but it gave her little time to work—something she always did when traveling by air. Still, confident Ryan would handle last-minute details before boarding the red-eye, she relaxed into her seat, case notes in her lap. At the moment, however, the investigation's main players were taking a back seat—what she really needed was a Cliff Notes version of fashion design. *I wish there were such a thing*, she thought as she flipped through pages of research Ryan gave her a few days prior. *I like wearing the clothes, but I don't know crap about making them . . .*

One thing immediately obvious was the required pace for their investigation—not enough time to breathe. Big Four Fashion Weeks were approaching, allowing little time for attending the shows, conducting interviews, and everything else needed for a successful investigation. After Paris, they were off to New York—then, London and Milan, then back to Paris. Seldom did she question her ability to keep up, but, as she studied their itinerary, time constraints smacked her in the face.

This is going to be hell . . .

His fingers caressed the fabric, its feel and look like gossamer wings. "C'est magnifique," he whispered to himself, a satisfied smile tugging at his lips.

Basile knew instantly it was the final fabric he needed for the Paris show—the design played in his mind for months, but, when assistants brought him possible textiles, none seemed right. But, what he held with his fingertips was perfection. "Ten yards," he ordered his assistant.

She nodded. "Anything else?"

"No—delivery within the hour!" With a slight, dismissive wave, he turned, electrified by the excitement of creating his final design. "Now, go . . ."

Moments later he sat, alone with nothing but visions of his new creation. He had little time, but, in his mind, there was nothing he couldn't accomplish. Then, he remembered his meeting with Colbie Colleen. *Of course, I must cancel!* Urgently, he picked up his cell to call the woman who could, possibly, reveal hidden solutions to his problem—yet, he hesitated. *Can I not do both?*

An interesting question—and, dilemma.

By early afternoon, she checked into her hotel, and it wasn't long until Colbie was fully immersed in the case. Her meeting with Duchon wasn't until the following day, allowing much needed time—but, there was something bugging her, yet she couldn't bring her concern to life. It was a feeling, really, experience nudging her to pay attention, yet nothing was defined.

On her tablet, she stared at the headshot and accompanying photos of Marguerite Villanova, a favored model of top-name designers—except Basile Duchon. According to insiders, her disassociation from him was an odd turn of events, reasons for the split purposefully veiled. In some circles, there was talk of his hurling the blackball with such force, her career was in jeopardy—but, within weeks, such gossip proved a false assumption. Even so, she was somewhat tarnished, stepping down a few rungs on the typically unbalanced fashion ladder.

Colbie tapped the screen. The model's bio popped up and, as she read, there seemed nothing out of the ordinary about Villanova's climb to fame. A girl of ordinary means, the only thing setting her apart from friends and classmates was her scrawny, towering height—as a freshman, she was five feet ten and, by her junior year, an inch over six feet. In heels?

She could play basketball with the best of them.

It was during the first year of university her life took a decided turn. Someone snapped a photo of her and, by a bizarre, circuitous route, it landed in the hands of an agent for the cream of the crop, most respected modeling agency. From there?

University was on hold.

Marguerite's entry and subsequent meteoric ascent within the fashion industry was that of legend, prompting models' tongues to wag, their gossip targeted and designed to sting. Of course, they knew there was more than a modicum of a chance Marguerite would hear, but that was what they wanted, wasn't it? Ultimately, however, Marguerite's choice was to ignore, not allowing it to burrow in like a tick in early spring.

The more Colbie read, the more she realized intricacies of the fashion world were cutthroat. It was no secret there were dens of iniquity cloistered deep within—places few were allowed to go, and the thought of infiltrating was daunting. *But*, she finally conceded, *if I have to go that route, I will . . .*

It would, however, require precision planning.

As she contemplated possible scenarios, her cell buzzed, Ryan's face popping into view. "Hey—what's up?"

"Nothing—I'm packed, and ready to go. I'm embarrassed to say I have as much stuff as you . . ."

Colbie laughed. "Never again can you give me crap about my luggage!" She shifted her weight as the tablet screen faded to black. Another tap to bring it back to life. "I've been thinking . . ."

"Dangerous. About what?"

"Our case—my gut tells me this is going to be long and involved."

"And . . . that's bad, how?"

"Well, it's not 'bad'—but, when I was sitting here a couple of minutes ago, tuning in on Marguerite Villanova . . ."

Ryan interrupted. "She's the model, right?"

"Yes. As I was saying . . . when I tuned in to her, I got a heavy feeling of illicit activity—mob stuff, or something similar." She paused. "Like she's involved in it, somehow . . ."

"I remember reading what people thought about her—but, the bigger picture is she's only a model. In many respects, that doesn't account for much—I wouldn't think a model would have anything to do with the industry's nefarious underpinnings . . ."

"Nefarious underpinnings?" A dramatic pause. "Wait a minute—have you been reading Merriam?"

"Very funny—I can bust out some good vocabulary when the situation calls for it!"

"Indeed. Anyway, I want to take a closer look at her . . ."

"When's your meeting with Duchon?"

"Tomorrow afternoon . . ."

"Do you want to meet before?"

"Of course—if my gut's right, we need a plan."

Ryan was quiet for a moment thinking how dangerous their investigation could be. "And, strategy . . ."

CHAPTER

2

He stood in front of the size two dress form, staring, arms crossed. *It must be perfect*, he thought as his fingers suddenly and nimbly draped cascading fabric across the form's left shoulder. Again, he stood back, assessing. "No! No!" His French accent echoed in the nearly barren room, hardwood floors bouncing sound at various angles. *Perhaps it is the lighting* . . . yet, sun streamed through floor-to-ceiling windows, bathing the studio in natural light, creating an early morning, delicate softness. It was Duchon's favorite time of day—when his creativity soared, freeing his mind from unwanted chains and shackles.

Still, something wasn't right. Disbelieving the fabric was causing his anxiety, he swept it off the form, allowing it to float and drape through his fingers. *No, no—the fabric is perfection* . . . Again, he carefully manipulated the silk, allowing it to fall as if it had its own will, its texture mesmerizing. More uniform than traditional silk, the fabric he held in his hands had an odd, interesting translucency—one he hadn't previously seen. In truth, it was a wonder he had the opportunity to work with it, at all—not only was it incredibly expensive, availability, for him, was next to nil—a punishment of sorts. No one, of course, knew of it and, at one point in his career, he thought of going the black market route, ultimately deciding the risk wasn't worth it. But, to have it in front of him at that moment?

Indescribable.

Duchon turned his attention to the large cutting table, pattern paper, rotary cutters, and scissors having their own, individual place. Each time he used one, he put it back in the exact same spot, an action many considered OCD.

Others considered it nuts.

But, it worked. Eccentricities fostered personal control, and he was master of his domain—perhaps the most important facet of his life.

Behind him, sunlight illuminated sketches and photographs bringing his winter collection to life—but, it was the final look of the show that was most important. The design making those lucky enough to attend, gasp at its beauty . . .

It will, he promised himself, *be my crowning glory* . . .

"I have to admit, it was nice to take a flight that didn't take the majority of my day . . ." Ryan stood in Colbie's hotel room, surveying her digs. "Your room's nicer than mine . . ."

She glanced at him with the appropriate amount of disdain. "They're the same . . ."

He grinned, telegraphing he was pulling her leg. "Then why does . . ."

"Ryan!"

"Okay, okay!" He took off his coat, throwing it on the nearest chair. "Where are we? You're seeing Duchon today, right?"

"Correct—this afternoon."

"Have you decided on a specific approach? I mean, the guy's a recluse except for showing up and claiming his fame at the fashion shows—someone like that can't be all there."

Colbie nodded. "Creative disposition, I suppose . . ."

"Creative disposition, my ass—you and I both know that kind of behavior isn't normal . . ."

"For us, no—for him, it might be the most normal thing in the world." She paused, looking at him. "There are a whole bunch of people, Ryan, who don't think or act like us—does that make them wacko?" Again, she paused. "I don't think so . . ." For some reason, his comment rankled her, but, instinctively, she knew he didn't mean anything by it.

"No, of course not—but, you can't go into your meeting thinking you're going to meet someone who's slightly quirky—you have to plan for something else, no matter how remote the chance."

Clearly, Ryan wasn't going to let it go. "You're right," she conceded. "I promise I won't go in with preconceived ideas about who Basile Duchon really is . . ."

"That's all I ask . . ."

Suddenly, an uncomfortable silence took root, setting them on edge with a heaviness neither could explain.

Colbie waited for Duchon's driver at the hotel entrance, eagerly anticipating meeting one of the world's top fashion designers. Ryan's earlier comment didn't dissuade her excitement, yet it did impress upon her she needed to be careful.

At precisely two-thirty, a nondescript SUV parked at the curb, the driver hurrying to meet her. "Ms. Colleen?"

Colbie nodded. "Yes! And, you are . . ."

"Francois—just Francois!"

Colbie couldn't help matching the young driver's infectious smile. "Well, Just Francois—I'm ready, if you are!"

Within minutes, the hotel faded from sight as Francois drove three blocks, then pulled into a well-hidden underground garage. "Is there something wrong," Colbie asked.

"No, no—we are here!"

She scanned her surroundings from the car. "This is it? My, that didn't take long!"

Francois grinned as he opened her door. "Very few know of this location—my employer prefers it that way." His accent was thick, some words more difficult than others.

He remained at her side as they headed for a well-disguised elevator. "I can see why not many people know this is here," Colbie commented, her unease beginning to mount.

"Basile Duchon takes no chances . . ."

Colbie nodded. "I can see that . . ."

As the elevator doors closed, Francois pushed two buttons. "Going down," he said with a smile.

Moments later, Colbie stood in front of the designer, stunned by what she saw—a diminutive man, a pallid pallor tingeing his skin with odd shades of yellow and blue, undoubtedly a result of life underground. His appearance didn't track, though—photographs of the designer didn't resemble the man standing before her.

"Monsieur Duchon . . ." Colbie extended her hand.

He smiled, yellowing teeth the result of years of smoking. "Mademoiselle Colleen—please come in!"

"Thank you . . ." Colbie accepted graciously, her eyes scanning every inch of the room as she stepped into the designer's studio.

Without a baseline, she had no idea what to expect— certainly not an expansive room bathed in sunlight from every direction, each wall lined with luxurious fabrics, as well as the simplest cottons. "This is stunning!"

Duchon beamed, his pride obvious. "Thank you—this is where I do my best work . . ."

"I can see why!"

"Please—follow me." He cupped her elbow gently with his hand, guiding her to the back of the main room. "I have a lovely sitting area . . ."

Lovely, indeed. A small, designer glass table was the only thing in the room, accompanied by two, elegant chairs. "Please—make yourself comfortable!" His invitation was warm. Honest.

After a few moments of getting settled, Colbie took the lead. "I confess I'm at a loss as to why I'm here, Mr. Duchon— so, why don't we begin there?"

Basile smiled. "Yes, yes—I think that's appropriate. Well, Mademoiselle Colleen, to be as succinct as possible, it's my opinion the fashion industry is no longer pristine."

"I'm not sure what you mean . . ."

"Undoubtedly, you researched me before arriving in Paris—so, you're aware of my humble beginnings. It wasn't until later in life, I reached my zenith . . ." A long sigh. "Sadly, the industry I love is no longer one guided by dedication and perfection. Design. Creativity. It is one of blood and money, and success is no longer guided by honesty and truth."

Genuine sadness signaling deep caring crept across his face as he spoke, Colbie noticing every movement he made—but, she said nothing.

"Designers are made," he continued, "and, no longer is it possible for someone like me to climb the ladder to the top rung. If one is not chosen, there is never a chance . . ."

"Are you saying the industry's . . . rigged?"

The sadness in his eyes deepened. "Without doubt, Mademoiselle Colleen . . ."

Colbie was silent, her mind ticking through possible scenarios. "Well—first, I'll appreciate your calling me Colbie—may I call you Basile?"

He smiled, leaned over, and patted her hand. "That will be lovely . . ."

For the next three hours they sat, discussing and planning, and, by the time Basile escorted her to the door, both were clear—with Duchon's help, Colbie and Ryan were to infiltrate the fashion industry.

What she would find, both were unsure.

"I think we need Kevin here," Colbie commented as she and Ryan settled in for a planning session.

"I've been thinking the same thing—from what you just told me about your meeting with Duchon, I don't think we can be without him . . ."

Decision made and a few cell calls later, Kevin was scheduled to arrive the following day. "Thanks for letting him bunk with you . . ."

"No problem—now, let's get to it. Where do you want to start?"

She focused on her notes. "When we parted, Duchon was preparing to make appropriate calls that will get us in the door . . ."

"Okay—clearly, this is an undercover gig. Lay it on me—who are we supposed to be?"

"Top-name fashion bloggers—at least, for me. You're going to be a vlogger—that allows us to have cameras."

"I don't know the first thing about cameras!"

"Neither do I—but, Kevin does. He'll give you a crash course as soon as he gets here . . ."

"If that's the case, why don't you have him be the vlogger—I can be your manager. Or, something . . ."

"That's . . . not a bad idea!"

"Well, it sure as hell makes more sense to me—besides, I'm good in supporting roles."

Colbie shot him a grin. "Yes, you are—but, I have a feeling I'm going to need you for much more than that . . ."

"Gut feeling?"

"Pretty much—when I was meeting with Duchon, as soon as we started talking about the case, I got an image of dress shears . . ."

"I have no idea what dress shears are . . ."

"Really long scissors designers use . . ."

"So, what about them?"

"At first, the scissors were closed—then, they opened slowly, and one of the blades fell off." Colbie paused. "There wasn't any sound of its landing on a hard surface and, when I looked down, it was stuck in the floor."

"Okay . . . any idea of what it means?"

"No—but, you know as well as I, my visions are random, and it's up to me to put them together . . ."

"Was that the only one?"

"So far, yes . . ."

"Well, that doesn't give us much to go on—so, I'm for forging ahead with a plan."

"Same here—the first thing we need to do is have Kevin create bios for us, making sure they're on the Internet in obvious places. Of course, he'll create a website . . ."

"I don't know—if you're a blogger, anyone looking you up will expect to see a blog, or two."

"Good point. Maybe Kevin can rig it—whenever someone clicks on the page, there's an error . . ."

Ryan grinned. "That just might work!"

CHAPTER

3

*R*yan laughed as he put one piece of luggage in the rental car's trunk. "This is it? You're making me look bad, you know . . ."

"It's something I learned from my dad—'take a little, learn a lot,' he always said."

"Smart man . . ."

Within the hour, both sat with Colbie, ready to strategize and plan the particulars. Ryan filled Kevin in on the bios he needed to create, as well as a shell fashion blog and website.

"Names," Kevin asked, glancing at both of them.

"Good grief! With everything else we've been thinking about, it never occurred to me to pick names!" Colbie focused on Ryan. "Well? Any ideas?"

"Let me think on it for a minute . . ."

"I would if we had an extra minute to waste . . ." She turned her attention to Kevin. "We had to do something similar when we worked a case in Cape Town—it worked pretty well."

"Were you ever found out?"

"Well—it turned out to be a rather sticky situation. But, for the most part, the scheme gave us time we needed to investigate . . ."

Kevin nodded. "Whatever names you choose, it has to be quick. What you're asking me to do isn't easy—and, it's going to take time . . ."

"You're right. Okay . . . how about Valentine? That's it—just Valentine for me, and . . ." She thought for a few moments. "Cyril . . ."

"What?" Ryan shot her a look.

"Cyril—what's wrong with it?"

He glanced at Kevin. "Well—nothing, I suppose. It's just kind of weird . . ."

"Don't forget, we're going to be anything, but normal— this is the fashion industry. Anything goes . . ."

"Okay—Cyril, it is. Just first names for both?"

Colbie turned to Kevin. "What do you think? What will be easiest for creating profiles for both of us?"

"Without last names, it will be much harder for anyone to dig deep . . ."

"But, you'll have just enough about us to answer nosy questions, won't you?'

Kevin nodded. "Count on it . . ."

"Perfect—how long will it take?"

"Give me twenty-four hours . . ." He glanced at both of them. "Anything else I need to know before I get started?"

Colbie grinned. "Just one more thing . . ."

"What's that?"

"You're going to be Cyril . . ."

After considerable discussion, they decided makeovers were in order—Colbie was recognizable, and she couldn't take a chance. "Valentine," she repeated to the stylist. "That's it—just Valentine." She grinned, thinking of Francois.

Moments later she rang off as Ryan knocked on her hotel room door. "Unfortunately, we have to meet a little later," she announced as she slipped into a pair of loafers. "I have an appointment with a makeup artist and hair stylist in thirty minutes. And, I have no idea where I'm going . . ."

"I'll tag along—we can talk on the way."

"Perfect—but, there's something you need to know . . ."

Ryan knew that look. "What . . ."

"You're getting a makeover, too . . ." Colbie waited for his reaction. "Did you hear me? You're getting a different style, too . . ."

"Oh, yes—I heard you. But, I've been with you long enough to know arguing isn't going to get me anywhere . . ."

"Excellent choice!" She paused. "Have you heard from Kevin?"

"A couple of minutes ago—he's done."

"Good. I hope he's ready to go . . ."

"Go?" Ryan glanced at Colbie, noticing a slight smile. "Makeover?"

"Yep . . ."

Colbie checked the address twice as the cab driver circled the block for the second time. "I know this is right,"

she murmured as she scanned several buildings. "Please pull over—we'll find the address!" She smiled warmly, hoping the driver didn't take offense to his not locating where she needed to go. But, it wasn't his fault—when Colbie suddenly recalled her conversation with Francois, she understood instantly the driver wasn't meant to find it. Basile Duchon provided the makeup artist and hair stylist and they, too, were undercover.

The driver complied and, within five minutes, they stood in front of a small door, overgrown with unruly trees and shrubs. "This is it . . ." Although there was no address to cue them, Colbie was certain they found their mark.

And, indeed, it was so. For nearly three hours, runway quality makeup and hair stylists created three personas, complete with professional headshots.

Celeste stepped back, eyeing Valentine from head to toe. "It is perfect!" She lead Colbie to floor-length mirrors. "Magnifique? No?"

Colbie gasped as she stared at her reflection—there was an edge to her style she found pleasing. "Oh, yes, Celeste! This *is* perfect!" She turned slightly, peering at the mirror from over her right shoulder. Celeste obviously knew what she was doing—spiky, red hair was styled to perfection, her makeup daring and unique. Trendy, army green, drop-crotch pants gave Valentine a hip, fashionable vibe, accompanied by a black leather jacket that felt like butter. Designer flats allowed her the opportunity to run, should she have the need.

As she turned to her left, Ryan and Kevin emerged from their separate salons. "Cyril!" Caught slightly off guard, Colbie realized they hadn't created a name for Ryan. "Liam! You look fabulous!"

Both men grinned, taking turns in the mirror as Colbie thanked the stylists. After a brief goodbye, she headed for the door, slipped on designer sunglasses, then turned to Ryan and Kevin. "Shall we?" There was no mistaking her dramatic flair.

Ryan glanced at Kevin, rolling his eyes. "Oh, brother!"

Laughing, they climbed into the cab Basile ordered, each enjoying the opportunity to make the most of their new identities.

"How long . . ." Armond Coniglio glanced away from one of the most elegant fabrics ever created.

"Three weeks . . ."

Neither spoke as they processed everything needing to be done. "I trust models are in place . . ."

"All, but one."

It was a response he didn't want to hear. "Who?

A pause. "Marguerite Villanova."

Coniglio said nothing—it was a mistake he hoped the model wasn't foolish enough to make. "That places her in a precarious position, does it not?" He turned to face the man he paid handsomely to keep secrets.

"As far as I know, she's still on the roster. I will consider her so, unless I hear otherwise . . ."

Silence.

Then, a change of topic. "The truth—do you think anyone will know?"

Luca Russo thought carefully, weighing his boss's question. "No," he finally answered.

Armond sighed heavily as if relieved from chronic burden. "That is good . . ." He thought for a moment. "Bring the lovely Marguerite Villanova to me . . ."

"Now?"

It was a question not needing an answer.

With New York Fashion Week only three weeks out, Colbie needed to infiltrate the industry as quickly as possible—that meant packing up, and heading to the States.

"Let's go over what we need to get in the door . . ."

Kevin nodded. "I have everything in place—all of us will have entrance badges, and we'll have free roam."

Ryan glanced at Colbie, then focused again on their neophyte partner. "How did you swing that?"

"Duchon—did I forget to mention he sent a messenger with all pertinent information?"

Ryan chuckled. "Well, yeah—it would have been nice to know . . ."

"When do we arrive?" Colbie pulled out her cell, tapping its calendar app to life.

"Day after tomorrow—it's the best I could do."

"Actually, I think that's perfect." Colbie was quiet for a moment. "It's been a whirlwind since we got here, and the less time we spend among people who saw us before our transformation, the better." She glanced at Ryan. "What do you think?"

"I think you're exactly right—it's probably best if we lie low for the remainder of our time here. Only room service, don't you think?"

"I completely agree . . ."

"And," Kevin added, "our flight is a red-eye—hopefully, it won't be packed."

Colbie looked at each of them, deciding whether she should include Kevin when discussing her visions. Finally, she opted for truth. "You've done a remarkable job, Kevin—and, we appreciate your jumping in as if it were nothing."

"No problem—what better way to get my feet wet?"

"That's true—anyway, it's clear you have everything under control." She paused. "So, I think it's only fair I'm honest with you . . ."

Kevin glanced at Ryan. "Okay—about what?"

"My visions . . ."

"I'm not sure I understand . . ."

"Well, before you arrived in Paris, I had a vision when I was talking to Basile Duchon . . ."

Kevin was silent.

"And," Colbie continued, "the first vision I had while in Paris was one of dress shears . . ."

"Those long scissors?"

Colbie glanced at Ryan with a slight smile. "Yes—so, when I was at Duchon's studio, I had a vision as he was speaking. Dress shears appeared in my mind's eye, then one side of the scissors fell off—and, when I looked down, it was stuck in the floor like a throwing knife."

Kevin swallowed hard. "What does that mean?"

"Well, that's the tough part. I don't know, but I do think it's a warning . . ."

"A warning of what?"

Colbie shrugged. "That's just it—I don't know. Yet . . ."

At that moment, Kevin had a decision to make—act is if everything were cool, or admit Colbie's abilities scared the crap out of him. It didn't take him long to opt for the first. "Will you let us know when you figure it out?"

Colbie and Ryan laughed. "You'll get used to it," Ryan commented as he stood. "And, now—I bid you farewell and goodnight. I'm pooped . . ."

Moment's later, Ryan and Kevin were on their way to their room, leaving Colbie to dream of unpleasant things.

She didn't tell either of them about the blood.

CHAPTER

4

The nearly nine-hour flight proved uneventful, and it wasn't long until they checked in at the hotel— one of New York's finest. It was one of many perks of which Basile Duchon insisted. "Besides," he commented to Colbie the day before they left Paris, "how else should I spend my money?"

Colbie made a mental note to inform him of their arrival as she slipped the key card into her room's lock. As she entered, a stunning bouquet of flowers on the small coffee table greeted her, their scent filling the room. *Good heavens,* she thought as she pulled the small card from its envelope. *Who on earth sent these? Basile?*

She read the card, one word perfectly placed in the center . .

Valentine?

What? She flipped the card over—nothing.

Again she read the message, instantly understanding its malevolent intent. *What the hell?* As she held the card in her fingertips, a negative energy coursed through her, as if a portend of things to come. How anyone knew of her arrival was interesting—but, knowing her pseudonym? Only she, Ryan, and Kevin knew. *Kevin was to make all media live after our arrival in New York . . .*

Slowly, she eased onto the couch's plush cushions, staring at the flowers as images leapt to life in her intuitive mind. As she watched, she was aware of—things—but, all were veiled, not offering a clear view, or clean perspective. It were as if a pale mist obscured the focus of her vision, causing Colbie to doubt what she thought she saw.

How long she sat, she wasn't sure, but her visions faded when Ryan knocked on the door. "Hold on!" She quickly tucked the card in her jeans pocket. *Later,* she thought as she headed for the door.

"Liam! How wonderful to see you! Please, come in . . ." No time like the present to begin the façade.

"Val!" Before he crossed the threshold, he kissed her on both cheeks. "You look fabulous!"

Colbie stepped aside as he entered, scanning what she could see of the hallway—no one. "Please, come in . . ."

Ryan busted a huge grin the second the door closed. "How'd I do?"

"You played your part like a true master!"

Ryan eyed the bouquet. "Who sent you flowers?"

Colbie plucked the card from her pocket, handing it to him. "I have no idea . . ."

"Who knows your name is Valentine? Kevin wasn't supposed to release any media until tomorrow . . ."

"I know—no one, as far as I recall."

"I'm calling him . . ." Seconds later, the called connected and, after brief conversation, Ryan clicked off, shaking his head. "It wasn't him—the media launch is scheduled for midnight."

Colbie held out her hand. "I want to keep it in a safe place . . ." Again, she flipped the card in her fingers. "When I opened the card? I was flooded with visions . . ."

"Anything we can use?"

"Not really—everything looked as if I were looking through something opaque. I couldn't make out anything else . . ."

Ryan took off his coat, throwing it on one of the chairs at the small dining table. "Weird—are you going to tell Kevin?"

"I thought of that—but, because I didn't see anything clearly, there's really no reason to tell him."

"Agreed—I kind of have the feeling your abilities freak him out a little."

"Well, I'll figure it out—dinner?"

"I thought you'd never ask!"

Although Fashion Week was still a few weeks out, Colbie wanted to meld into the behind-the-scenes crush of workers to get a feel for things. Those enmeshed in the fashion circuit traveled from event to event making certain tiny details weren't a reason for failure, and the high tempo, fast-paced atmosphere was already in full swing.

"This is weird," Ryan commented as they showed their badges—courtesy of Basile Duchon—to the security guard stationed at the entrance.

Colbie glanced at him, smiling, still not used to his new look. "Have you ever been to a fashion show," she asked as soon as they were out of the security guard's sight line.

"One—my sister was modeling an ice skating outfit when I was in third grade, and my mom forced me to go."

"How old was your sister?"

"Six . . "

After thinking about it for a moment, Colbie laughed, patting him lightly on the back. "I think it's safe to say you know nothing . . ."

"Other than what I watched and researched online? You're right . . ."

"Well, get ready—from what I understand from Basile, it's wild!"

Rounding a corner and heading toward what sounded like construction activity, a young man approached, clutching a a spiral binder. "Who are you," he asked, flipping through several pages of forms, then stared at their press and photographer badges. "Valentine what?"

"Just Valentine."

He eyed her skeptically, then turned his attention to Ryan. "You? Who are you?

"Liam . . ."

He squinted, paying particular attention to Ryan's interesting style.

"Just Liam . . ." Ryan offered before anyone asked.

Colbie picked up on their greeter's detailed personality, his frustration mounting. "Our names should be on the list. Guests of Basile Duchon . . ."

"Him, too?" The young man pointed to Kevin.

"Cyril? Yes—the three of us are guaranteed carte blanch access."

"Just Cyril?" Clearly enjoying his smart-ass comment, he was about to say something else when, suddenly, his eyebrows arched. Pushing up his glasses with his index finger—it was the only one with nail polish—he checked off their names with a flair. "Here you are!"

Colbie smiled warmly. "Excellent! Thank you . . ."

Apparently, there was nothing more to discuss as their greeter pushed past Kevin on his way to the main doors.

"So . . . that was weird." Ryan scanned the massive main stage, memorizing faces of workers who might keep their eyes open. Believing behind-the-scenes personnel often had pertinent information, he preferred to get cozy with them while Colbie and Kevin took on designers and models.

With a plan firmly in place, Colbie and Kevin headed backstage, while Ryan split off toward the working guys. "It's interesting," she commented to Kevin, "no one seems to pay attention to anyone else." She stood for a moment, watching. "Well—is your camera ready?" She glanced at him, enjoying the slightly disconcerted look on his face.

"Ready as I'll ever be . . ."

Colbie set her sights on a thirty-something woman with long, blonde hair. "Let's go . . ."

As they approached, there was no mistaking the concern—or, perhaps, fear—on the woman's face. "Excuse me . . ." Colbie waited a moment for a response. Nothing. "Excuse me . . . are you Maria Carvante? I have an appointment with her in ten, and no one seems to know where she is . . ." Of course, there was no such person, but she hoped the ploy would work.

"No—I don't know who she is."

Colbie softened her tone. "My boss is going to be pissed if I screw this up . . ." She paused. "Maybe you've seen her— really tall, about twenty—she's one of the models for Fashion Week." Another pause. "What's your name? You and Maria really look alike!"

That did it. "Madelinne . . ." She, too, squinted at their badges, making Kevin wonder if the print were too small— either that, or everyone they met needed glasses. "Oh! Press!" Instantly, her tone changed, and she quickly afforded Colbie a few moments of her precious time.

Recognizing Madelinne's interest in the possibility she may get a little good press from her, Colbie took advantage of a perfect opportunity. "I know you're incredibly busy— but, by any chance, do you have time for a quick interview?"

Madelinne glanced at her watch. "I think so!"

Things couldn't have worked out better.

Colbie turned to Kevin. "This is Cyril—he's my photographer, and he's been with me for years! You'll love his work!" She paused, scanning the backstage area. "Is there someplace we can talk without all the noise?"

"There's a lounge—at least, that's what we call it. All of this will change the closer we get to the show . . ."

Within minutes, both sat in folding chairs, Kevin fussing with his camera while Colbie set up the shot. "I want this to be natural, Cyril—I want to show what New York Fashion Week is all about."

Kevin nodded. "Got it . . ." He focused his video camera on Madelinne.

Colbie grinned. "When you told us your name, I knew I recognized you—in fact, when I saw you at a show last spring, I thought you were one of the models!"

Madelinne blushed. "Milan? No—I'm not tall enough. Maybe that's why I got interested in designing . . ."

And, so it went. The few minutes with Madelinne turned into a little over an hour, Kevin playing his role perfectly.

"So . . ." Colbie glanced purposely at her watch. "I know you have to get back to work—but, I have one more question, if you don't mind."

Madelinne nodded. "Sure . . ."

Colbie's tone was serious as she broached the first question pertinent to her investigation. "Now, I know how you got into this business," she began. "But, now that you've been at it for a while, what would you change?"

Colbie noticed the young designer glance at Kevin. "Cyril—cut," she ordered, then turned her attention again to Madelinne. "No one will ever know . . ."

"It's just that . . ." Madelinne's voice faded to a whisper.

"Just what?"

No response. "I won't betray your confidence," Colbie promised, and it was one she could make easily—other than her investigation team, there wasn't a soul who would hear Madelinne's words.

After a moment's hesitation, Madelinne looked at the floor, then at Colbie, her eyes brimming with tears. "You have no idea what it's like . . ."

Colbie reached for her hand, giving it a gentle squeeze, knowing she caught the designer at the height of frustration—which was good for Colbie. "Tell me . . ."

A sniffle. "Well . . . I always thought being a fashion designer would be the coolest thing in the world. But, now— it's nothing, but a nasty environment."

"You had to know that, though—it's been that way for decades."

"I did—but, I didn't think it would be so bad. When I went to Italy at the beginning of my career? I was so excited to be around names I heard from the time I was little—Coniglio. Duchon. Hallberg . . ."

"You should have been excited! So, what happened to change that—did someone do something?"

"Not at first—but, somehow, I got in the good graces of Armond Coniglio, and I managed his sample room."

Colbie was having a difficult time putting two and two together, so she finally asked the bombshell question. "What happened, Madelinne?"

A brief silence. "Armond Coniglio arranged a disastrous falling out with one of the best international models . . ."

"A falling out with whom?"

"Basile Duchon . . ."

"Who was the model?"

"Marguerite Villanova . . ."

Colbie was quiet for a moment, thinking. "Let me see if I have this straight—you're saying Armond Coniglio arranged for a falling out between Basile Duchon and Marguerite Villanova. Right? One meant to ruin careers?"

"Exactly . . ."

"Why?"

"Because Armond wanted Duchon out of the way—and, he figured shaming him within the design industry was the way to get him out of his hair."

Another silence. "So, what was the 'shaming' thing about? For that to happen, obviously, Armond Coniglio had something on Basile Duchon. Do you know what it was?"

"No—all I know is Armond's plan worked."

Colbie figured it was time to reaffirm her position within the fashion and design industry. "I know about Marguerite Villanova's problems—it was a pretty quick fall from grace when her story hit the wires."

Madelinne nodded. "Except there wasn't a speck of truth to any of it . . ."

"You mean Coniglio wanted to take down Marguerite, *and* Duchon?"

"As far as I could tell, Basile Duchon was the main target. Marguerite was nothing more than . . ." The designer hesitated, searching for the right word.

"Collateral damage?"

Again, Madelinne nodded. "That's about the size of it. Nothing more, nothing less . . ."

Chapter

5

*R*yan sat back, focusing on Colbie after watching her complete interview with Madelinne—at least, until Kevin pulled the plug. "This is what Duchon was referring to . . ."

"I know—it's really the crux of our investigation. But, what doesn't make sense to me is why would Coniglio want Basile Duchon's designs never to walk the runway again?"

Ryan thought for a moment. "Design theft? It sure as hell wouldn't be the first time. Or, maybe . . . we're looking at it from the wrong perspective—what if Duchon has something on Armond Coniglio? Then what?"

"Well—that certainly would change the trajectory of our investigation. Do you think it's possible?"

"Anything, at this point, is possible—what we have to consider is what's probable."

Colbie smiled, recalling when she and Ryan worked together in Cape Town. The years following graced him with confidence and savvy investigative intelligence—all abilities Colbie knew he had.

"So—moving on. What about you? Anything worth talking about?"

"Not really—although, there was one person who seemed a little too full of himself."

"Name?"

"All I know is his first name—Rob. He was in charge of bossing everyone around—and, he apparently took his duties seriously."

"Meaning . . ."

"He was a total ass!"

Colbie grinned. "Is that you talking, or someone you talked to?"

"Both! It didn't take a genius to see this guy was high on power . . ."

"What was the gossip among the workers?"

"Most were pretty tight-lipped. I felt it was rude to ask, but I imagine their wages are pretty good, especially if they're union. But, for the few who were sick of their boss's dictatorial attitude, they didn't give a damn who was listening . . ."

"Interesting—of course, it's no secret about the rampant abuse throughout the industry. If I recall correctly, not too many years ago, models got together to have their voices heard regarding the situation—and, I think that was the beginning of changes."

"You're right—I read several articles on it. The guys I talked to, however, weren't working directly for this Rob guy—but, if required to, some of them would have refused. One guy said he—Rob—was out of the Italy industry, but I can't verify it. Or, I haven't yet, I should say . . ."

Colbie thought for a minute, cycling her conversation with Madelinne through her mind. "An abuse angle might make sense given what we now know about Armond Coniglio."

"I thought of that . . ."

Again, Colbie was quiet, mentally working through something. "Okay. What do you think about this—we're only a little less than three weeks out for the New York show. Next, is London . . ."

"And . . ."

"How do you feel about spending a little time in Italy as a well-credentialed fashion photographer?"

"You mean *before* London?"

"Yep—I'll keep Kevin with me, you go to Italy, and we'll meet up in London."

"Sounds good—except, how am I going to get close to Coniglio?"

Colbie grinned, then headed for the suite's fridge. "Leave that part to me . . ."

Tall, willowy, and elegant, Marguerite Villanova glided through custom designed French doors, caring little she wasn't properly announced. "I understand you summoned me . . ." Without waiting for a response, she took her favorite place on the antique couch. "Now what?"

There was a tone in her voice Armond didn't like, or appreciate. He cocked his head to one side, not taking his eyes from hers. "It has come to my attention there is question about your participating in New York . . ."

Marguerite crossed her legs, folding them close to the couch. "I don't understand your concern . . ." She watched Coniglio's upper lip twitch slightly, enjoying every second of his trying to maintain composure.

"You understand perfectly, my dear. May I remind you this is a dangerous game you're playing?"

"From whose perspective, Armond? Yours?" A smile played on her lips, knowing she did, indeed, have the upper hand—a situation Armond Coniglio would never admit, or entertain.

The designer crossed to the small bar, poured himself a drink, then sat in the chair across from one of the world's favorite international models.

The slight didn't go unnoticed. "Why, Armond— nothing for me?"

He took a sip, then smiled. "Oh, my dear—I wouldn't say that . . ."

Luckily, snagging a seat on the red-eye to Milan wasn't a problem—a good thing since Ryan wasn't wild about being crammed into his seat for nearly eight hours next to someone he didn't know.

"Let me know when you arrive," Colbie requested. "Kevin and I are doing recon at Armond Coniglio's shop—then, this afternoon, I have a phone meeting with Basile." She watched him check his ticket a second time to make sure everything was a go. "And, tomorrow, we start attending the soirées leading up to the big event . . ."

"Lucky you . . ."

"It'll be interesting, that's for sure!"

"Will Kevin be with you?" Ryan didn't care for the idea of leaving Colbie to fend for herself, although he knew she was perfectly capable of doing so. Still, a little nudge of protectiveness settled in, giving rise to an all too familiar feeling.

"Everywhere I go . . ."

Finally, she watched him hoist his backpack onto his shoulders, then stride down the passengers' boarding bridge. Suddenly, he turned and waved, flashing the grin she knew so well.

In that moment, all she could hope is he wouldn't leave her, too.

There was an elegance Colbie expected as she stepped across the threshold into Armond Coniglio's Fifth Avenue flagship store. Tastefully appointed in hues of grey, black, and white, it was clear Coniglio spared no expense.

"Good morning—welcome to Armond's!" A middle-aged, stunningly dressed woman smiled as Colbie and Kevin walked through the door. Trained to allow patrons to shop at their leisure, she remained at an Italian marble desk with nothing on it but a vase of flowers, and an elegantly styled telephone.

"Holy shit," Kevin muttered as Colbie made her way toward the designer shoes. "I can't afford to buy a tie . . ."

"Neither can I . . ."

Taking their time, they explored, until Colbie felt it was time to strike up a conversation with the woman at the desk. "This is lovely—how lucky you are to work here!"

The woman who dripped money smiled. "Thank you—I am, indeed, fortunate!"

"I can't imagine wearing such fabulous clothes . . ." She eyed the woman's stylish, winter dress. "That looks fabulous on you . . ." She paused. "What's your name?"

"Giorgia . . ."

"Well, Giorgia—you look absolutely wonderful!" Another pause. "Have you ever had the opportunity to meet Armond Coniglio? I can't imagine what he must be like in person!"

"Yes. He's lovely . . ."

It was then Colbie detected a slight Italian accent—a fact piquing her interest. "Are you from Italy?"

Giorgia glanced around the shop, even though Colbie and Ryan were her first customers of the day. "Yes, although I've been here for many years . . ."

"I love Italy—especially Northern. It's so beautiful . . ."

"Indeed—I lived there during my childhood."

"Did you come to the States when you left?"

"Oh, no—Milan. That's where I met Armond . . ." She smiled, a coat slightly crooked on its hanger catching her eye. "But, my time there was short. Soon, I left for the States—and, here I am!"

Colbie grinned. "That's why your accent is so subtle!" She hesitated before asking her next question. "What's he like—Armond, I mean? His vision for design is absolutely breathtaking!"

"He certainly has a creative eye—the best, really."

"I agree—did you work for him?" She glanced at Kevin. "Wouldn't that be fabulous, Cyril? Having an opportunity to work with Armond Coniglio?" She didn't give Giorgia time to answer, hoping her feigned excitement would be enough to keep her talking.

Kevin didn't miss his cue, agreeing with just enough interest to be convincing.

"Well," Giorgia commented, "it certainly was one of the most interesting times of my life! And, to answer your question, Armond is a man who knows what he wants—yet, he's willing to take chances."

Colbie listened intently. "You mean risks?"

"Well . . . yes."

Suddenly, Kevin checked his watch. "Val—we have to go."

Colbie glanced at him, then at Giorgio. "I'm so sorry— I'd love to talk more, but Cyril is right. There's a Fashion Week event beginning at noon, and I have to get dressed!"

Within moments they were out the door, walking briskly away from the store. "What was that all about," she asked as they stood at a corner waiting for the light to turn.

"I'm sorry—but, when I noticed her expression change, it seemed like she was getting a little suspicious."

"Giorgia's?"

"Yeah—it was weird."

Colbie turned to look at him. "You did exactly the right thing . . ." In that moment, there was no doubt Kevin was an asset to their investigation. "Thank you . . ."

Luca Russo stepped into the showroom from a back entrance. "Who were you speaking to," he asked, watching Colbie and Kevin cross the street.

"Her friend called her 'Val'—his name is Cyril."

He glanced at Giorgia, then back at the street, mentally noting Colbie's and Kevin's direction. "What did she want?"

"Nothing—nothing, but small talk. Only complimenting the store, as well as Armond . . ."

Russo was quiet, his sixth sense on high alert. "She asked many questions . . ."

Giorgia was silent, fully aware she was being chastised.

"What did you answer?" His tone edged with impatience, he glanced around the showroom as if someone were lurking among its hangers.

"Nothing of importance—we spoke of Italy's beauty. That's all . . ."

Russo's impatience escalated. "You spoke of Italy for ten minutes?" He paused. " For ten minutes you discussed it?" His gaze turned scathing as he focused all of his attention on her. "I think not . . ." With that, he turned, heading toward the store's front door. Then, he turned again to the woman he was beginning not to trust. "You would do well to keep your conversation with patrons to a minimum . . ."

After a few hours' sleep, Ryan reached out to Colbie, filling her in on the flight, hotel, and his proposed schedule for the following day. "I did my research on the plane, and I want to interview designers who haven't hit the big time . . ."

"Good idea—I'm getting the impression Armond Coniglio isn't the greatest guy on the planet, and there have to be a few dissatisfied underlings." Colbie hesitated. "Madelinne said she managed the sample room operations, so maybe that's a good place to start . . ."

"Check. I can drop her name to see if anyone bites . . ." Ryan paused, again thinking about leaving Colbie alone in New York—well, alone, except for Kevin. "Did you make it to Armond's on Fifth like you planned?"

For the next half hour, Colbie filled him in on her conversation with Giorgia. "If it hadn't been for Kevin's detecting a change in her expression . . ."

Ryan chuckled. "Good man, Kevin! I knew he'd look after you!" The second the words left his mouth, he regretted them, knowing she'd pounce.

"Look after me?"

"Well, yeah—for now, he's taking my place!"

Colbie wasn't sure it was the time for a personal discussion—it had been a tiring day, and she didn't have the energy. "I'm going to let that go—for now!"

"Good—I was about to get myself in hot water!"

"Oh, you already did . . ." As much as she didn't want to admit it, Colbie enjoyed the banter, and having Kevin as a substitute?

It wasn't quite the same.

By the end of the week, Fashion Week events were kicking into high gear, offering Colbie an opportunity to rub elbows with the world's tops designers. When bringing Basile up to speed on the investigation, he stressed the importance of her attending. "Strip away the false, and you will see the true," he promised, knowing everyone there would be armored with insincerity.

Colbie promised she would and, as they were about to end the call, Basile offered additional caution. "There will be a man—Luca Russo—who spearheads Armond Coniglio's operation."

"What about him?"

"I have always suspected he was instrumental in effecting my runway demise . . ."

"On behalf of Armond?"

"Of course! Who else?"

Colbie listened, visions streaking through her mind, but she paid attention to only one—an image depicting the cover of the book, *The Judas Tree*. A warning. An intuitive symbol she knew intimately, it hadn't failed her in years of investigating. The first time it appeared, she lacked understanding—but, after reading the novel, there was no doubt about it's warning of despicable sin every time it appeared. *Do I know the whole story*, she wondered as she clicked off.

As she recalled every discussion with Basile Duchon, it became clear she knew little, certainly by Duchon's design. *Perhaps Ryan's right—maybe Duchon has something on Armond Coniglio, and he's using us as pawns . . .*

The more she considered the possibility, the more she realized she'd been too trusting when meeting with Duchon for the first time—the only time. The thought of being set up as players in someone else's game didn't sit well, and she began to recognize subtle shades of truth. She would, of course, heed Basile's warning . . .

But, doing so would be on her own terms.

CHAPTER

6

*S*tar-studded parties didn't get underway until fashionably late and, when Colbie arrived shortly after ten, she stepped into the true world of fashion—a world few knew, or had the opportunity to see.

Basile's connections provided seamless access and, by eleven, she already made the rounds consisting of nothing, but small talk. *Time for a change*, she thought as she accepted a glass of champagne.

She scanned the room, recognizing only a few from pictures on the Internet, or fashion magazines. Kevin snapped photos, never focusing on one person until a man walked in the door, and everyone turned to look. "Who's that," he whispered to Colbie.

"Luca Russo. I recall Basile's warning me about him before we left Paris . . ." researching Armond Coniglio's right-hand man hadn't proved difficult and, from what she learned, he was a man used to the camera, enjoying the limelight.

But, instinctively, Colbie knew he was a man of shadows.

It wasn't until nearly an hour later, she had an opportunity for conversation. "Mr. Russo?"

Luca Russo made no apology for looking her up and down, assessing her trendy designer outfit from head to toe. "Yes?"

Colbie extended her hand. "I'm Val . . ." She rattled off the title of her blog, but he paid no attention, so she motioned for Kevin to join her. "Cyril—will you please shoot a few of Mr. Russo and me?"

Immediately, Kevin began snapping pics, listening closely to Colbie for a possible veiled directive.

"This will be fabulous for my readers," she gushed. "It's not too often I have my picture taken with such a handsome man . . ."

Always one to accept a compliment, Luca Russo smiled, his stolid demeanor softening, if only a bit. Together, he and Colbie posed for Kevin as Colbie offered to send him prints. "I assume you're staying nearby—I can have Cyril drop them off with the concierge . . ."

"That won't be necessary . . ."

"Oh, come on—who wouldn't want a picture of moi?" She offered her most tantalizing smile, a gesture breaking the ice—something that rarely happened with Luca Russo. But, there was a flair about the fiery redhead with cropped, spiked hair he appreciated and, when considering the possibility of seeing her again, he found the thought alluring.

By the time he bid goodnight to his host and hostess, Colbie was planning surveillance, starting with his hotel. In between champagne and broiled, lobster-stuffed canapes, she and Kevin planned the following day. "I brought a wig," she informed him. "He'll never recognize me—especially from a distance."

"What about me? He knows exactly what I look like—if he gets a gander at me, then what?"

"Good point—I doubt he's going to be paying too much attention to what's going on around him. If you stay in the background, I think we'll be okay . . ."

Kevin wasn't so sure. "What about you? We can conduct surveillance from a distance, can't we?"

Colbie nodded. "Yes—for now, I just want to watch where he's going. It's time I know the real players . . ."

Kevin did a double take as Colbie met him the following morning, blonde wig and all. "Too much," she asked with a grin as she joined him for breakfast.

"In New York? Hell, no!"

Their order for ham and eggs finally with the server, conversation turned to the day's surveillance. "The most important thing," Colbie advised, "is to stay out of sight—take as many shots as you can, but act as though you're taking pictures of the city."

"That shouldn't be too hard—especially in the fashion district. I seriously doubt anyone will be paying attention to me . . ."

"Agreed—and, while you're doing that, I'll keep my eyes peeled for Russo. So, make sure you're close to me at all times—I don't want to be shouting at you from across the street."

Within forty-five, they stationed themselves outside of one of New York's most famous hotels. "How much do you think it costs to stay there," Kevin asked as he zoomed in and out, making sure of the camera's settings.

"I have no idea, but I'm pretty sure neither of us can afford it . . ."

"On another note," Kevin mentioned between sips of coffee, "Ryan called last night . . ."

"He called you?"

Kevin grinned. "Oh—didn't he call you?"

Colbie laughed, enjoying Kevin's sense of humor. "No, he didn't call me!"

"Oh . . . that's too bad."

"Very funny—what did he have to say?"

"Not much—he said he was going to call you, but realized it was too late. So, he said he settled for me . . ."

"Sounds like Ryan . . . did he mention anything about his investigation?"

"A little—he said he's meeting a designer tomorrow. Rumor has it this particular fashion diva has a bone to pick with Armond Coniglio . . ."

Colbie stared at Kevin, mid-bite. "How does he know that?"

"He didn't say—but, he sounded pretty amped about talking to her."

Colbie was quiet, thinking about Ryan's mystery interview. "Well," she finally conceded, "he'll handle it well. He always does . . ."

It turned out they waited much longer than anticipated for Luca Russo to show his face in public—then, at precisely two o'clock, he strode through the hotel's door, the doorman smiling at him as if they were old friends.

"Obviously, he stayed at the hotel before," Colbie observed as Russo shook the doorman's hand.

Kevin eyed the two men through the camera lens. "You're probably right—they seem pretty chummy."

Moments later, Russo strode down the street toward the fashion industry's main venue. "Let's go—try to keep an eye on him!" Colbie shot across the street just as the light flashed its warning, watching him turn the corner. "Do you see him," she asked as they reached where he disappeared.

"Nope—he's gone."

"Damn! All that time waiting, and we got nothing more than a glimpse of him . . ."

Kevin checked his camera to make certain he put the lens cap on. "Well—maybe it wasn't a waste of time. Since he knows the doorman at the hotel—maybe we can get something out of him."

"Maybe—but, I'd be willing to bet a doorman isn't going to say anything about hotel patrons. If it ever got out? So much for his job . . ."

Kevin grinned at her, shifting the camera. "If your conversation with Giorgia is any indication, I'll be you can get anyone to talk . . ."

Colbie leaned against the cold, concrete wall of a small shop, hands in her pockets, watching people walking by. "I don't know—but, there's something about Luca Russo I don't like. And, I don't trust him . . ."

"All that from meeting him at a party?"

She leveled her attention on him. "Oh, yes—and, more."

"I hope I didn't call too late . . ."

"That's okay—I was only sleeping."

Colbie listened for a moment, unsure if Ryan were joking. By the time she and Kevin made it back to the hotel after losing Luca Russo—as well as attending a fashionably late lunch to welcome international fashionistas to New York—there was little time to squeeze in a call. "Then, it's a good thing sleep isn't important . . ."

Ryan laughed, flicking on the lamp on the nightstand. "I was still up—after the day I had, I barely had time to eat!"

"Midnight snack?"

Again, he chuckled. "You know me too well . . ." He grabbed his sandwich from the hotel room fridge, then settled on the bed. "So—you. How was your day?"

Colbie filled him in on her conversation with Luca Russo at the party, then their brief surveillance the following day. "Unfortunately, we lost him . . ."

"He shouldn't be too difficult to find—it's a pretty good bet he'll be at the show venue."

"That's what I figure—especially since he's Armond Coniglio's right-hand guy."

"Speaking of Armond Coniglio . . ."

"You mentioned talking to designers . . ."

"Yep—three, to be exact. I dropped Madelinne's name and, interestingly, no one bothered to check my credentials."

"Seriously?"

"I know—I would have thought there'd be tougher security."

Colbie thought for a minute, recalling Basile's underground design studio, as well as where he arranged for their makeovers. "As I understand it, a sample room is the nuts and bolts of any designer's operation—you'd think they'd keep it under lock and key."

Ryan took a bite of his sandwich, chasing it with a swig of milk. "Well, lucky for me they didn't. And, it was a lot different than I thought . . ."

"In what way?"

"How many people worked there, and no one really paid attention to what anyone else was doing. So, I managed to get in a couple of private conversations . . ."

"I can't believe they talked to you . . ."

"They didn't while they were at work. But, I followed them to a local watering hole when their shifts ended and, after a few drinks, they were more than willing . . ."

For the better part of an hour, Colbie and Ryan dissected his conversations with the women working in Coniglio's sample room, the only usable information being the mutual hatred of their boss. "From what I gathered, he's an ass . . ."

"Somehow, that doesn't surprise me . . ."

After a few more minutes, they rang off, both promising to stay in touch daily even if it were only by text—Colbie wasn't comfortable with too much time elapsing without touching base. *At least I can trust him to run his end of things,* she thought as she kicked off her slippers, and slid into bed.

Within minutes, her body relaxed into the contours of the mattress, relieving stress from the day. But, it wasn't to be a night filled with dreams, visions, and intuition . . .

It was a night filled with dreams of Luca Russo.

"I can't believe it's Fashion Week—it seems like we just got here . . ." Kevin hoisted his camera bag to the other shoulder. "Where should we set up?"

"Duchon made sure we have preferential treatment—front row."

"Is that really where you want to be? There will be photographers everywhere, and the chance of your getting a little press is pretty high . . ."

Colbie stopped checking her messages to see if there were anything from Ryan, giving Kevin her full attention. "Holy . . . I never thought about that, but you're right." She paused, thinking. "The last thing I need is being front and center at an international event—even though focus will be on models and celebrities, it would be just my luck to wind up on the front page of a magazine . . ."

"So—what do you want to do?"

"You should be in the front—no one is going to know you, so you'll get lost in the crush of photographers."

"What about you?"

"I'll watch from several rows back—that will give me a chance to watch people and, if I'm lucky, get behind the scenes . . ."

"I don't know—there are so many different events, it will be easy to lose track of you."

"Just make sure you have your phone, and it's charged. The next week and a half is going to be busy, not to mention exhausting. I'll do the same—that way, if we get separated, we can agree on a place to meet."

Kevin recalled his recent conversation with Ryan. "Don't let her out of your sight," Ryan warned. Still, he was in no position to argue.

Colbie noticed his hesitation. "Are you okay with that?"

"Yep!"

"Good—let's head for the main runway. That's where mainstream designers will show . . ."

Within the hour, both were in their respective positions and, precisely at nine, the first runway show was underway. As predicted, high rollers, celebs, and critics claimed their seats in the first few rows, the latter scribbling notes furiously as they critiqued each look. Colbie paid particular attention to those attending while Kevin snapped photos of models, as well as those in the audience.

And, so it went for the first week of the show—Kevin learned more about fashion and modeling than he wanted to know as Colbie's intuition was in high gear. Throughout the week, Valentine and Cyril were on display, no one the wiser of their true vocations as nearly one hundred individual runway shows took place.

By the time the second-to-last day rolled around, both were exhausted, ready and looking forward to a little R & R. "I don't know about you," Colbie commented to Ryan as they discussed the following day's events, "but, Kevin and I have a couple of days before our flight to London. He may have something on his list of things to do, but I plan on catching up on sleep . . ."

"Probably a good idea—the good news is you only have tomorrow left, and you're done with the first show. By the time you get to London, you'll have the kinks worked out, and you'll know exactly what you need to do."

Colbie was silent for a minute, thinking about the previous week. "It just occurred to me—you know who was missing at this show? At least, so far . . ."

"Give me a clue . . ."

"Marguerite Villanova . . ."

"Did anyone ever mention her name?"

"Now that I think about it . . . no."

"Well—maybe she wasn't slated to work New York."

"Or, any other of the shows—there's something about the whole, Villanova, Duchon, and Coniglio thing that bugs me. My gut says they're the main players in our investigation, but I'm not sure in what way . . ."

"What about Hallberg? Was he at New York?"

"Yes—but, I got the feeling he doesn't have anything to do with our investigation even though he's in the top five international designers . . ."

"That narrows it down—now what?"

Colbie considered what she had to accomplish on the last day of New York Fashion Week. "As of this moment, I don't see anything out of the ordinary—taking into consideration, of course, how much I don't know about the industry. I'm inclined to think the first major show of the year isn't where feathers will be ruffled . . ."

Ryan agreed. "Did you see Duchon?"

"Briefly, but we didn't connect—we thought it would be better to have no communication."

"Probably smart. What about the other guys?"

"Coniglio blew in and blew out—there was the usual press around him, not to mention body guards."

"I can believe that after what happened to Versace . . ."

"Precisely . . ."

After solidifying travel plans, they clicked off with the agreement to touch base the following morning in case there were changes. Colbie couldn't get Marguerite Villanova out of her mind, and intuition was telling her to pay attention.

You just landed on my radar, Ms. Villanova. I hope you're ready . . .

CHAPTER

7

*M*arguerite stood still as Luca Russo fussed, barking instructions to Coniglio's top staff designer. Before leaving Milan, Armond's wishes were clear, and Russo was to make certain they were carried out flawlessly.

So far, so good.

Of course, there was plenty of press regarding Coniglio's designs, but it was backstage whispers at private parties amping anticipation beyond previous runway shows. Gossip in full swing, those in the know speculated about Coniglio's latest collection, purportedly using fabrics not previously unveiled. To make things more intriguing, there wasn't much interest in what was on the fabric—print or solid—it was the fabric itself.

Russo eyed Villanova with a critical eye. "Have you gained weight, my dear? You're looking a little . . . pudgy."

Marguerite smiled slightly, knowing his comment was meant to sting. "Just the opposite—I'm nearly a pound lighter since we last met. With your detailed perspective, I'm surprised you can't tell . . ."

"Perhaps it's not the weight I'm noticing . . ."

"Meaning?"

Luca motioned to the sewer working on last minute fit issues for the final look of Coniglio's collection to take a break. "I hear things," he continued. "I hope you're not placing yourself in a precarious situation . . ."

Marguerite's eyes grew cold as she focused her attention on him. "I'm not a fool, Luca . . ."

"There's talk . . ."

"I can do nothing about what people say about me—it's none of my business." She glanced at her reflection in one of the many full-length, backstage mirrors. "Perhaps you would do well by following suit . . ."

A flush of anger crept up Russo's neck as he listened to the model's disrespect—a clear indication of a shift in their relationship. "As I indicated," he continued in an effort to put a cap on his anger and frustration, "there is talk. Not only of you, but of Madelinne, as well." He paused. "What do you know of it?"

"Madelinne? Or, the talk . . ."

"Both . . ."

Marguerite continued admiring her silhouette in the mirror. "Before I answer your question, I need to know one thing . . ."

"And, that is . . ."

"Why do you want to know?"

Luca could do nothing but sputter at the audacity of her question—perhaps, in a different situation, he would properly punish her for such insolence—for the moment, however, it was prudent to let it go. "It has come to my attention Madelinne was spending time with someone from the press . . ."

"So? Everybody spends time with the press during fashion week . . ." Again, she turned her attention to him. "I don't understand your concern . . ."

Luca said nothing, thinking about the conversation he had with one of his . . . scouts. Talk circled back to him about Madelinne's spending time with a member of the press—someone with red, spiky hair, and a style that would make anyone look twice. "Do you know of her?"

"No."

"Perhaps, you know her name . . ."

Villanova looked at him with disgust. "And, perhaps, you are hard of hearing." She paused, relishing her position. "Now, let's continue with the fitting, shall we?"

In all of his years of managing Armond Coniglio's fashion empire, never had he been spoken to in such a manner. In that moment, he realized he had two issues—

first, Marguerite Villanova was a problem with which he must contend. The second?

The woman with red, spiky hair with only one name . . .

Valentine.

London was as Colbie remembered, although she hadn't been there since she and Ryan worked together on the Cape Town case.

A fading winter greeted them with fog and drizzle as she and Kevin stepped off the plane, Colbie unsure if Ryan would be there to meet them. "Keep your eyes peeled," she commented to Kevin as they headed toward baggage claim.

Twenty minutes later, they stood at the curb, waiting for their partner. "This isn't like him," Colbie commented, scanning cars lining up to retrieve passengers.

"Did you talk to him?"

"Of course—yesterday morning."

"Not since then?"

"Nope—he had things to accomplish, and we were getting ready to leave New York. There wasn't time . . ."

"Maybe you should text him . . ."

Colbie nodded. "If he's not here . . ."

Just then, a sleek, stunning, gunmetal grey SUV pulled up to the curb, it's window's tinted so no one had a chance to see things meant to be private. "This must be someone important," Kevin commented as it slowed to a stop.

"No surprise—if you ever have the chance to people watch here, I suggest you take it!"

The passenger window rolled down slightly. "Get your asses in here! It's freezing!" Then, it rolled down completely, Ryan's face in full view, grinning like the Cheshire cat.

Kevin glanced at Colbie. "Are you kidding me?"

Colbie tried not to smile. "Please—don't encourage him."

"Well? Are you going to stand there all day?" Ryan popped the trunk, then focused on Kevin. "It's nice having another man around—you can do all the heavy lifting!"

Within five, he pulled away from the curb, heading for their hotel. "Do you remember the digs we had the last time we were here?"

Colbie nodded. "Of course, I remember—it hasn't been that long!"

"Well, if you liked that place, you're gonna love what Duchon arranged . . ."

Kevin barely paid attention to conversation as he stared out the window at places he'd never seen. Although he enjoyed full partnership with Colbie and Ryan, there was no question his contribution to the firm was on a lesser scale—so, as they pulled up in front of their hotel, he made a personal promise to learn as much as he could from them.

"Hey! Kevin! You home?" Ryan peered at him in the rearview mirror.

"Yep! Just thinking . . ."

"Well, stop it—we're here!"

Kevin grinned, then unbuckled his seatbelt. "Yes, Sir!"

Ryan and Kevin decided to bunk together, even though Duchon had no problem springing for three suites. "It's good we're on the same floor . . ." Ryan checked his room number, then looked down the hall. "We're at the end, I think . . ."

"Let's meet up in an hour," Colbie suggested. "Do you want to eat in, or out?"

Ryan glanced at Kevin. "I'm all for staying in—we have to be at the venue tomorrow morning, so I need my beauty sleep . . ."

"Miss Valentine?"

Colbie stared at the massive bouquet of flowers nearly obscuring the young bellhop. "Good heavens! For me?"

"They are, indeed!" His speech slightly Cockney, his smile revealed a space between his two front teeth. "Where would you like them?"

Colbie stepped aside, allowing him to enter. "How about on the coffee table?"

Moments later, she tipped him, waiting until he was gone before reading the card. Carefully, she extracted it from its envelope, her breath catching as she read the beautiful, hand-scripted message . . .

Valentine?

Instantly, she recalled the flowers she received in New York. *I know I kept the card,* she thought, as she rummaged through her messenger bag. Within in seconds, she compared the writing. *They're not the same!*

She grabbed her cell, then tapped Ryan's speed dial number. "Are you in your room?"

"Yep—why?"

"I have something to show you—five minutes?"

A minute shy of their agreed upon time, he knocked on her door. "Okay—I'm here," he advised when she opened the door. "What's up?"

Colbie handed him the card.

Quickly reading the message, he flipped it over. Nothing. "Weird—is this from the same person who sent you flowers in New York?"

"That's what I thought—but, when I compared the writing of the two messages, they're different . . ."

Ryan thought for a minute. "That may not mean anything, though—it's easy to change handwriting."

Colbie pointed at the script. "That's not every day handwriting—it's calligraphy, and it's not easy."

"Still . . ." He glanced at her. "Do you know anything about calligraphy?"

"I know enough to know these aren't the same . . ." She compared the two cards, side by side.

"I don't know crap about it, either—but, I'm betting there are more styles than one. You know—kind of like art. You should remember that from our Cape Town case. No two pieces are alike . . ."

Colbie tightened the belt on her bathrobe, then headed for the suite's small kitchen. "Coffee?"

"Do you have to ask?"

She laughed, filled two mugs, then joined him on the couch. "I hope it's not too strong . . ."

"I'm sure it's fine," he assured her as she set the mug on the coffee table in front of the flowers. "So—what do you think? Same person?"

She nodded. "My gut tells me it is, and someone is trying to throw me off the trail by using a different style of calligraphy." She paused. "I think you're right about that . . ."

"I like being right first thing in the morning," he admitted as he took a sip. "Geez! Hot!"

"Sorry . . ." Again, she looked the cards, this time holding them close, comparing not only the writing, but the ink, as well. "You don't happen to have a magnifying glass, do you?"

"Not on me . . ."

"That's okay—I have mine." She dug to the bottom of her messenger bag, finally extracting a small, high quality magnifying glass.

Ryan watched, shaking his head as she slid the glass from it's case. "Of course, you do . . ."

A quick lens swipe, then she lowered it over the writing, adjusting it slightly to get the best perspective. "I don't know why you're so surprised," she commented. "I am a handwriting analyst, after all . . ."

"I get it—so, what do you see?"

Colbie handed him the magnifying glass, and two cards. "Look at the 'V' in 'Valentine' . . . they're different. And, the pastosity . . ."

"The what?"

"Pastosity—it's kind of like the thickness of the writing. It has an equal thickness for up and down strokes, and it looks a little muddy. These two look similar . . ."

Ryan adjusted the magnifying glass for a clearer view. "I don't know . . ."

"Seriously? Look again—you can see the ink is slightly different, as is the shape of the 'V.'

Ryan held the card closer to the glass. "You're right— but, they're awfully close. Besides, like I said, handwriting changes—you taught me that when we were in Cape Town."

"You're right—it does change. But, I'm beginning to think whoever wrote this made a concerted effort to make them look similar. There's a difference in the pressure . . ."

"They did a pretty damned good job, if you ask me!"

Colbie nodded. "They did—and, anyone who isn't trained in handwriting analysis probably wouldn't see the slight differences . . ."

Ryan placed the cards on the table. "If that's the case, it might indicate someone who isn't familiar with your background . . ."

"Or, maybe he—or, she—knows my background, but failed to consider my noticing."

Ryan thought for a minute, then picked up the card Colbie received in New York. "The question is why is someone sending this to you?" He paused. "When you received the first one . . ." He flicked the card with his fingertip. "You thought it was from Basile . . ."

"That's right—nobody else knew I was there."

"At least, that's what you thought. After seeing this one, though . . ." He picked up the second card. "You can't still think it was a nice gesture from the guy who hired you . . ."

As they considered possibilities, Colbie's cell chirped. "It's a text from Kevin. He wants to know if he can join the party . . ."

Ryan laughed. "He's such a weirdo . . ."

"Yes—but, he's our weirdo!" She answered a quick yes and, moments later, there was a knock on the door. "That was speedy," she laughed as she stepped aside, inviting him in.

"That's because I was standing outside your door when I sent the text . . ."

"What if I said no?"

Kevin shed his coat, placing it on the back of a chair. "I knew you wouldn't . . ."

In that moment, Colbie found the warmth missing in their partnership—the three of them were meant to be.

Kevin spied the flowers and cards. "You got flowers in New York . . ."

Colbie filled him in and, for the next hour, they tossed around ideas about the flowers, who sent them, and why. Finally, however, it was time to get to work. "Let's approach the London show the same as New York—Kevin and I have the hang of it, and our ruse worked pretty well."

Ryan nodded. "Works for me . . ." He paused, focusing on Colbie. "I didn't have a chance to tell you, but I have a meeting with the designer you met in New York. She agreed to meet with me for an interview . . ."

"Madelinne?"

"Yep—one and the same."

"How did you manage to get in touch with her?"

"Oh, I have my ways . . ."

Colbie glanced at Kevin, rolling her eyes. "Really? What ways would those be?"

"Well, remember the girls from Coniglio's sample room?"

"Yes—you had drinks with them after their shift."

He nodded. "That's right. I didn't mention it to you at the time, but I met one of them the following evening."

Colbie felt an anxious pang she didn't understand. "Just the two of you?"

"Yep—I figured she could tell me more. She was the chattiest one at the bar . . ."

"Are you saying she's the one who gave you Madelinne's contact information?"

"Email and phone . . ."

Colbie shook her head as if trying to rid her brain of cobwebs. "Okay—let me see if I understand you correctly. You managed to coax information from one of Armond Coniglio's sample room workers and, as a result, you're meeting Madelinne today."

"That's right . . ."

"Why?"

Ryan focused his full attention on her. "Because, after a few drinks, she mentioned Armond Coniglio's 'bitch in residence'—that's what she called Madelinne."

"Armond's worker called her that?"

"Yep—why, I don't know. But, I intend to find out . . ."

"From the sample room chick?" There was an edge to her voice, previously not there.

"No—from Madelinne. I figure a little schmoozing might just work . . ."

"What do you intend to learn?"

Ryan stared at the two flower cards for a second, then turned to Colbie. "Didn't she say how cutthroat the fashion business is?"

"Yes, but . . ."

"Well, doesn't it make you wonder why she said that?"

"Of course, it does . . ."

"Me, too—I have a gut feeling she was much more involved in Armond Coniglio's life than merely someone working in his sample room."

Colbie nodded. "You're probably right—especially after hearing what girls in the sample room call her."

"Well, at least one of them . . ."

"It's possible, however, there was bad blood between your girl and Madelinne . . ."

"My girl?"

Colbie laughed. "You didn't mention her name!"

"Oh. Right. Her name is Chiara—that's all I know."

As Colbie and Ryan worked through their individual thoughts, Kevin watched, feeling a little left out. "So, when are you meeting Madelinne?"

"Not until this evening . . ."

"What time?"

"Seven . . ."

Kevin picked up on Colbie's thoughts. "Dinner?"

Ryan nodded. "It will be a much better atmosphere for extracting information . . ."

Finally, Colbie commented. "I think it's a great idea—obviously, she doesn't have a problem talking about her former employer."

Ryan agreed. "That's just it—but, if my gut is right, I think there was much more to their relationship."

"While you're at it," Colbie suggested, "try to find out if she had some sort of feud with Chiara . . ."

"My thought, precisely . . ."

CHAPTER

8

*A*rmond Coniglio held an espresso cup with both hands, directing his complete attention to the woman who, at one time, occupied most of his time. "Just what do you expect to learn," he asked, "from this man you're meeting?"

"I don't know—but, I sense there is something."

"Then, you're doing nothing more than wasting my time . . ."

"Really? Is that what you think? Do you have any idea there's talk?"

Coniglio chuckled, then took a sip. "Talk of what?"

"You . . ."

His eyes narrowed as he considered the possibility of someone speaking behind his back. "I assume that's your reason for our impromptu meeting . . ."

Madelinne nodded, never taking her eyes from his. "I have a feeling things are about to change . . ."

Armond was quiet for a moment, deciding if his former sample room manager were worth the time and effort. "Who is speaking about me?"

"Chiara."

"How do you know?"

"I happened to be at the same bistro where she—as well as a few others from the room—met with a man. A man from the States . . ."

"So? I fail to see what such a gathering has anything to do with me . . ."

Madelinne pushed back her chair, placing her napkin on the table. "Perhaps you should pay more attention . . ." She rose, smoothing her skirt. "All I'm doing is alerting you to what could become a situation—if you choose not to heed my warning, then you are responsible for your actions. Not me . . ."

With those words she left him to ponder his situation. There were mounting indications of difficulties within, but, according to Luca, it was nothing he couldn't handle. *Do I trust you to do what is right, Luca?* A sip to calm his escalating anger. *Perhaps, it is time . . .*

Entry into London Fashion Week turned out to be easier than New York, Colbie's and Kevin's newfound familiarity with the industry allowing them to scrutinize aspects of the event they may have missed in the States. "There are over two hundred designers at all four events," Colbie commented as they headed for the main runway. "I'm playing my part, so be prepared to start snapping . . ."

Kevin shifted his camera bag to the other shoulder. "Check—let's hang here for a minute, so I can get set up." By then, he knew Colbie well enough to know a few minutes to herself allowed time she needed to tune in to what most couldn't see.

"How about if I meet you back here in five? I'll wander while you're getting your camera ready . . ." Without waiting for an answer, she struck out on her own, knowing full well it would be at least ten minutes before Kevin would have his camera ready to go.

As with the New York show, the venue was in full swing as she took note of those around her. Suddenly, she turned, cued by strong negative energy, its direct source unclear— but, there was no doubt someone she probably wouldn't like was nearby.

"You ready?"

Colbie whirled around. "Kevin! You scared the livin' crap out of me!"

"Sorry—I said your name, but you didn't hear me."

Colbie stood for a moment, attempting to pinpoint the direction of the negative energy. "My intuition is telling me there's someone we need to talk to—someone close."

Kevin scanned the backstage area. "Do you know who?"

"No. That's just it—I can't get a direction."

"Male, or female?"

"Female . . ."

For the next several minutes, both navigated through workers, designers, and admin assistants keeping a wary eye on progress. Even though designers—top name, or otherwise—didn't have much say about the inner workings of the show, they found it prudent to guard against surprises. Most assistants made sure everything was progressing as anticipated, reporting to their bosses on a daily basis.

"Wait . . ." Colbie stood still, watching a vision play out in her mind. "Blonde."

"What about those two?" Kevin pointed to two women at the farthest corner of the room. "They're blonde . . ."

Colbie glanced at him, nodding. "Follow my lead . . ."

Slowing as they approached, Colbie tapped into her intuition. "That's her . . ."

"Which one? Both are blonde . . ."

"The one on the left . . ."

Within seconds, Colbie broke into their conversation with an engaging smile. "I'm so sorry—I don't mean to interrupt . . ."

The woman on the left slammed her with a scathing glance. "Yes, you do . . ."

Stunned, the woman next to her offered an immediate apology. "Is there something we can do for you?"

The woman spewing negative energy was a silent warning for Colbie to steer clear—doing so, however, was an impossibility. She offered her hand. "My name is Valentine, and this is my photographer, Cyril . . ."

The well-mannered woman smiled, running her fingers through her short hair. "I'm Kara Vaughan . . ."

Colbie glanced at the woman she knew was going to be trouble. "And, you are?"

The woman cast an irritated glance, then addressed only her colleague. "We'll have to continue our conversation later . . ." Without acknowledging Colbie or Kevin, she walked away without so much as a second glance.

"She's really pissed," Colbie commented, turning her attention to Kara. "Again, I apologize for interrupting your conversation . . ."

"Don't think twice about her—she's been that way for as long as I can remember!" She smiled at Kevin. "I take it you're a reporter?"

"Is is obvious?" Colbie laughed as the negative energy began to clear. "Yes—I'm a style and design writer, and Cyril is the guy who captures the runway shows." Rattling off her credentials and website address, she left no doubt in Kara's mind she was the real deal—still, it might be prudent to check.

"So, what can I do for you, Valentine?"

"Well . . . I'm showcasing top, international designers, focusing on what happens behind the scenes." She paused, thinking it was time for a little name dropping. "I had the opportunity in New York to meet Luca Russo, and . . ."

"Luca? He's a lovely man!"

"Indeed! We didn't have much time to talk, but I can see how Armond needs him as his right-hand guy . . ."

Kara nodded. "They've been together for years, as you probably already know."

Colbie turned to Kevin. "Cyril—will you please snap a couple of pics of Kara and me?" She paused, shooting a smile at the woman who didn't know she was about to talk too much. "You don't mind, do you? I want to have great memories of each Fashion Week!"

"Of course not," she grinned, then hesitated for a moment. "You're not going to publish them, are you?"

"Good heaven's, no! It's just for my phone gallery . . ."

For the next few minutes, both women followed Kevin's directions for the best shots, and, finally, it was time to get down to business. "When I met Luca at one of the events in New York," Colbie commented, "I admit I was struck by his presence . . ."

"Presence?"

"Well, yeah—you know what I mean . . . he carries himself with a certain dignity not present in most men." She glanced at Kevin who was stifling a smile. "At least, he's not like most men in my life!"

Kara laughed. "Maybe it's because he's Italian!"

"Probably! Is Armond Coniglio the same?"

"Armond? Oh, yes—he runs a tight ship, and God forbid anyone who doesn't follow his directions. I always had the feeling Luca keeps him balanced, if you know what I mean."

Colbie nodded. "I do—and, I can see how Luca could be that influence." She paused, playing the moment. "I haven't met Armond yet, but I do have time with him toward the end of the show." She turned to Kevin. "Do you remember when my appointment with Armond Coniglio is?"

No hesitation. "Two o'clock on the last day . . ."

She returned her attention to Kara, smiling. "If I didn't have Cyril, I don't know what I'd do!" A pause. "What's he like—Armond, I mean. I've heard so many different things, but I make it a point not to take too much to heart until I meet him in person."

"Probably wise . . ."

"Do you know him well?"

"Well, I sourced fabrics for him before my current position . . ."

"Which is?"

"Marketing Director for Basile Duchon . . . "

Colbie tried to quell a surprised, choking cough. Granted, she was hired by Duchon to find out who was trying to take him down, but, it was in that moment she realized she walked into her case ill-prepared. She should have recognized Kara's name instantly—but, didn't.

"Basile? He seems like a wonderful man—but, from what I hear, it's next to impossible to get an interview with him!"

Kara grinned. "You're right about that! If you said you had an interview with him, I'd begin to wonder . . ."

As much as Colbie wanted to hear about her employer, it was clear her time with Kara was better spent talking about Coniglio. "I heard through the grapevine—as did nearly everyone in the industry—Duchon and Armond don't get along. Is that true?"

Kara thought for a moment, considering whether she should answer—but, the falling out between her current employer and her previous one was well-known, so what could it hurt?

"They used to—but, a few years ago, things changed. I wasn't in the thick of it, of course, because it was my position to source fabrics for Armond. Nothing else . . ."

"Were you the only one?"

"Sourcing fabrics? For the most part . . ." She paused. "Let's put it this way—Armond trusted me to bring him the best."

"You must have been traveling a lot . . ."

"Constantly—it was one of the reasons I decided to accept Basile's offer. I was exhausted, and things were beginning to change within the industry . . ."

"Obviously, you travel for Duchon—not as much, I presume?"

"Yes—I have people working for me to do most of the legwork. I try, however, to keep my fingers in the pie for the four Fashion Week shows . . ."

Colbie was quiet for a moment. "Do you mind if I ask you a question?"

Kara grinned. "Well, that depends on the question!"

Colbie matched her smile with one of her own. "I promise I won't ask you to divulge industry secrets!" A pause. "I have, though, always wondered what happened between Duchon and Coniglio. For as many years as I've been in the industry from the sidelines—as a writer—I don't recall there being such animosity between designers. Is that typical?"

"Typical? Hardly. Although, keep in mind you're working in an industry of egos beginning at the bottom rung of the ladder up to the top . . ."

"What do you think happened between them?"

"I'm sure I can't say—all I can tell you is their disdain for each other is consuming. Armond is relentless . . ."

"And, Duchon?"

"Cunning."

They agreed to meet earlier rather than later—everyone in the industry was used to keeping long hours and, during Fashion Week, they ramped up to the edge of exhaustion.

"I'm not surprised it's crowded," Ryan commented as he pulled out her chair at a small table "It's a good thing I could get a reservation!"

As Madelinne stood beside him, she realized they were nearly the same height. "This is one of my favorite places in London . . ."

"Same here—but, I confess, I've only been here once, and that was several years ago!"

"It probably hasn't changed too much!" Folding her legs elegantly under the table, she watched as he sat, then signaled the server, glancing at his dinner date. "What would you like to drink?"

"I'm good with a beer!"

"Ah—a woman after my own heart!" Moments later, the server was on her way, leaving them to settle into a what Ryan hoped would be an illuminating conversation. "So," he began, "what is it about the fashion industry that attracts you? Did you always want to be a designer?"

"Oh, yes! My mother bought me a sewing machine when I was nine years old . . ."

"That was it? You were hooked?"

As she was about to answer, the server returned with their beers. "That was quick! Shall we wait to order," he asked Madelinne, the server standing poised with her ticket book and pen.

"Let's—how about thirty minutes?"

Ryan nodded, waiting to continue their conversation until the server set her sights on a new table. "To . . . Fashion Week!" He offered the toast, their glasses barely clinking. "Back to what we were talking about—your first sewing machine . . ."

"I'm certain it was only exciting for me, but it was the start of understanding what I wanted to do with my life."

"Meaning?"

"Well . . . after I made my first skirt, I knew I wanted to be a designer. My mother told me I had to follow the rules—in other words, learning to sew using a pattern. But, I had different ideas, even though I discovered I loved pattern making . . ."

Pretending he knew what she was talking about, he listened intently. "Eventually, that's what led you to working with Armond Coniglio?"

"Many, many years later—yes." She cocked her head slightly. "What about you? Why did you decide to get into the fashion industry?"

Ryan chuckled, thinking the prep work he did before the case was going to come in handy. "Well—I'm not in the design end, as you know. I've always been interested in writing, and clothes—the two just seem to go together."

She looked him up and down, making no excuse for her interest. "You wear clothes well . . ."

He took a swig, hoping he wasn't blushing—and, if he were honest, he enjoyed the attention. "So—tell me. What's it like? The industry, I mean—you're out on your own as a designer, right?"

"Yes—I knew if I never took the leap, I'd wind up regretting it."

"That's the way it usually goes . . ." Ryan paused. "What was it like working with Coniglio? Some say he's great—others, not so much."

Madelinne sat back, resting her fingertips lightly on her beer glass. "Armond Coniglio is a mercurial man, conforming to whatever's necessary to get the job done."

Ryan's eyebrows arched. "What job needs doing?"

"Why, being the number one international designer in the world!"

"Ah! Ego."

"Indeed—and, the fact Basile Duchon occupied the coveted number one position? Well, it's safe to say it didn't sit well with Armond . . ."

"Is that why you decided to seek greener pastures?"

Madelinne eyed him. "I did no such thing—it was merely time I followed my life's dream. I realized I could never achieve success if I stayed under anyone's thumb—now, I have no one to answer to, but myself."

He watched as a coldness settled in her eyes, signaling a change of topic. "I researched you . . ."

"I'm flattered . . ."

"From what I know about clothes, you have what it takes—you can be a force."

She said nothing, enjoying the compliment.

Then, Ryan asked a question she'd never heard. "Do you think you can be a force?"

There was a tenderness in his question, her answer the same. "Perhaps . . ."

CHAPTER

9

On the couch, Colbie tucked her legs underneath her, arranging her bathrobe so they were completely covered. The frigid chill in London's winter air was etched in her brain and, on her current trip, she made certain to have hot chocolate in her room at all times.

The large mug warmed her hands as she considered disturbing elements of her investigation—the first being her not recognizing Kara Vaughan's name. For such a prestigious position, Colbie should have put two and two together at first mention—but, for her, such a mistake was unusual, and one she couldn't ignore.

As she warmed her soul with her favorite Belgian nightcap, thoughts wandered, eventually eclipsed by her intuitive mind. She closed her eyes for there was no fighting it—she couldn't if she wanted to.

But, that evening, there was something different about her visions—slow. Deliberate. Targeted. Usually, they sped in and out with barely enough time to get a good look. That time? She was meant to take notice.

She watched as two men sat at a table, their backs to her, obscured in shadow—who they were, she had no idea. Then, the tips of two daggers dripping blood, pooling into something she couldn't quite distinguish.

As quickly as the vision appeared, it was gone, but only after Colbie had enough time to peer into it's meaning. Surfacing, she intuitively knew lives were in danger.

The question was whose?

Ryan picked up his cell, then thought the better of it as he cycled through his evening with Madelinne. There was something about her he couldn't quite figure out, and he knew Colbie would ask. So, until he had something concrete, keeping mum except for the facts was probably a good approach.

As far as he could tell, Chiara's comments about Madelinne didn't measure up, and there was nothing about her to suggest she was difficult to get along with, or know. In fact, she was the opposite—he found her charming and delightful, as well as drop-dead gorgeous, and it was no surprise she was deeply enmeshed in the fashion industry. *She takes boho chic to a whole new level,* he thought, as he envisioned the woman who sat across from him for three hours—much longer than either anticipated.

It was the discrepancy between perception and truth he found disturbing, making him wonder why Chiara was so forceful with her opinion. She seemed nice enough, but, he suspected she might be much like a rattlesnake sunning on a dusty rock—watching. Waiting. *If that's the case, I need to watch my ass* . . . Still, he wondered if he were duped by his zeal to find out something important—if so, he was quick to realize he needed to spend more time with Chiara.

"Something's off," he muttered as his cell screen illuminated. *Colbie* . . .

He couldn't think of a time he let a call from her patch into voicemail—but, that evening? It was late, and he wanted to think about Madelinne. Chiara.

The disconnect.

"It's late . . ."

"I'm aware—but, something has come to my attention."

"It couldn't wait until morning?"

Armond Coniglio poured a glass of cabernet, savoring its fragrance before taking a delicate sip. "If it could wait until morning, you wouldn't be here now, would you?"

Luca Russo eyed him, detecting irritation in his boss's voice—and, the slight of not offering him a glass of wine didn't go unnoticed. "It seems you're displeased. Not with me, I hope . . ."

"Well, that remains to be seen—what's important is what I hear from the street."

"The street?" Russo chuckled at the thought of the great Armond Coniglio walking among the commoners. "The street doesn't become you, Armond—so, let's get to it. Clearly, you're struggling with something . . ."

Coniglio smiled. "Indeed. So, let me be brief—it's come to my attention the sample room isn't working to peak efficiency."

"I'm not sure I understand—production is exactly where it should be, especially before all Fashion Week shows."

"I know—that aspect of my business is functioning flawlessly. It's gossip from within serving as a stain upon my reputation . . ."

Luca Russo's expression set. "Gossip? About you?"

"Can you think of any other reason I'd call to meet so late at night?"

It was a question requiring no answer. "What's the gossip about? And, who is . . ."

"Spreading lies?"

Luca nodded. "I assume you know the source . . ."

Another sip. "I do. It's the bold, yet apparently stupid Chiara . . ."

Both men were quiet, each knowing there was nothing else to say. The problem?

Handled.

"I tried calling last night—you must have gotten in late."

Ryan grinned, recalling what time her call logged on his cell. "It wasn't that late . . ."

"Oh! So, you knew I called . . ." Colbie turned to look at him, playful accusation in her eyes.

"Busted!" Ryan grinned, then plucked a bagel from the bakery box. "I just wasn't sure what to make of my evening with Madelinne—and, I wanted to think about it before cluing you in on our conversation."

"Really? Interesting . . ." She eyed him. "So, tell me . . ."

For the next hour, they sat, discussing Ryan's evening, finally capping off the conversation with his advising Colbie he needed to talk to Chiara again. "But," he commented, "my gut says I can't waltz into the sample room . . ."

"Agreed. So, what do you have in mind?"

Ryan thought for a moment. "I want to set up a photo shoot at the sample room, if I can—and, you can interview a few working there, as well as Chiara. I can introduce you, and you can say you're writing an article from a behind-the-scenes perspective . . ."

"I can't imagine they'd let anyone with cameras in the door—the one thing I've learned in my short time in the industry is designers are a private bunch. God forbid if anyone allows the possibility of designs being copied, leaked, or whatever . . ."

"Good point." He was quiet, then glanced at Colbie. "Any ideas?"

"Do you have Chiara's phone number?"

"Really? You have to ask?"

Colbie smiled. "Just checking—if I were you, I'd call her to set up an evening for dinner. I can pretend to run into you, and you invite me to join you—which will be much to Chiara's dismay, of course."

"Makes sense—it will be interesting to get your take on her."

"What about Madelinne?"

Ryan's eyebrows arched. "I don't know—what about her?"

"Do you need to see her again?"

"Maybe. I haven't decided . . ."

Luca Russo was curious for only a second if such action were necessary. Of course, there were unpleasant aspects to his job, but none, he figured, above his ability to carry out orders—and, when Armond Coniglio made his wishes known, it was critical to make them a reality.

Still, it was an unsavory bit of business, one which he didn't enjoy. Even so, infidelity of any kind simply couldn't be tolerated, and it was within his job description to take care of such matters without notice, or fanfare.

It's what Armond expected.

He made certain the location was away from prying eyes, although there were a few moments of consternation. Chiara simply didn't understand why he was taking her so far into the country on such a blustery, winter's day no matter what he said, and it was her insistence regarding return to London cuing him it was time.

Although carrying out his plan was rougher than he originally anticipated, in the end, his execution was perfect.

Precise.

Even if someone does discover you, my darling, it's already too late . . .

"You met her?"

"Yes—recently. And, her photographer . . ."

Basile Duchon studied the new marketing director, appreciating and admiring his foresight for hiring her away from Coniglio. It was a maneuver unplanned, but, when word snaked throughout the design community, few eyebrows arched. Everyone knew Kara Vaughan was worth far more than Coniglio was paying her, so, when Basile made overtures, she listened.

The truth was she tired of Armond's heavy-handed approach to her expertise, micromanaging every facet of her search for world-class fabrics, and it was on the industry's undercurrent word reached those in the know. Within days of making known her wishes to consider other opportunities, Duchon offered her a deal she couldn't refuse.

"What do you think?" Although he suspected his employee knew of Colbie's true identity, it was best to maintain the façade.

Kara didn't answer for a moment, recalling the ten minutes or so she spent with the style and design columnist. "She seems nice enough—but, I think it's time you're truthful with me. Her name isn't Valentine—it's Colbie Colleen."

Duchon signaled no recognition, remaining silent while waiting to learn how much she knew.

"So," she continued, "why don't you tell me why she's snooping around?" Kara didn't take her eyes from her employer.

"What do you suspect?"

"Honestly, I'm not certain—but, I think it has something to do with Armond. He was the focus of her questioning . . ."

"I don't mind saying it disturbs me Ms. Colleen was so transparent. How did you learn of her identity?"

"A contact of mine in New York . . ."

"A name?"

"I'd rather not . . ."

"But, I think it's appropriate, don't you?"

Kara eyed him, momentarily considering she may have made the wrong choice—she wasn't about to be in a position where she didn't have a voice. "I think, for now, I'll keep that information to myself . . ."

An uncomfortable silence.

CHAPTER

10

*T*here's a sleazy side to every city. Every town. No matter the country, society's underbelly carries on business as usual among those who know the rules. It's where handshakes mean nothing, corruption is the norm, and anyone who forsakes the code of unspoken anonymity risks paying the ultimate price.

As the two men sat, a lingering scent of stale cigar smoke reminded each it was a place neither wanted to be—it was necessary, however, to maintain required privacy. Knowing the owner for over two decades, both knew their words would never leave the room—something upon which upper echelon designers insisted when greasing his palm.

"Thank you—I appreciate your attention to this serious matter . . ." Basile fidgeted slightly, his diminutive frame ill-fitted to the oversized armchair. "It has, I believe, reached the point when interference is on the horizon . . ."

Oscar Hallberg glanced at the behemoth of a man standing by the door leading to a nondescript alley. "Perhaps we should be alone . . ."

Duchon followed his glance. "Him? Not to worry—I pay him far more than he's worth, so I doubt he presents a problem." Duchon paused, his normally kind, blue eyes the color of steel. "So, I propose we get on with our business . . ."

Hallberg nodded. It was unwise to go against the French designer, and anyone with half a brain knew it. Although considered benign within most fashion circles, there wasn't one among them who wasn't aware of Duchon's calculated cunning. "Tell me, Basile—to what do I owe the pleasure?"

"It's come to my attention there's movement among the ranks—up and coming designers are talking too much, and those remaining behind the scenes are speaking about things of which they know little . . ."

"I heard . . ."

"It's only a matter of time before you, too, fall prey to his machinations . . ."

"You worry too much! I have no fear . . ."

"Then, you are a fool." Basile didn't take his eyes from the man sitting beside him in a matching mahogany, red leather armchair, only a small table separating them. "Armond Coniglio will stop at nothing . . ." He paused. "I know you agree . . ."

"That may be so, but I have no desire to ripple the waters at this time."

Duchon was quiet for a moment. He hadn't counted on Hallberg's pushback—an action he regarded foolhardy. "Anyone coming against Armond Coniglio tap dances on hot coals, his or her future uncertain. But, you know what he's done—surely you can't condone!"

"Of course not—but, at this time in my career, I consider it ill-advised to make a shift. I am perfectly happy where I am, doing what I do. What Armond Coniglio does with his life is of no concern to me."

Basile stood, limbs trembling. "But, what of me? I didn't deserve what he did! How can you carry respect for such a man?" A drop of spittle oozed from the corner of his mouth.

"I don't recall saying I respect him—but, you must agree, Basile, you're playing with fire. You are certain to lose your fight . . ."

"Basile Duchon never loses!"

Hallberg eyed him, knowing the designer's words held no truth. "Ah! But, you already have . . ."

It was a comment slamming Duchon with such force, he sat down, taking a moment to regain his composure. "He had no right . . ." His voice caught as he recalled the total devastation of his career.

"Perhaps, it is time for you to move on—you're again amongst the greats, although your rank is lessened. Is that so bad?"

"To most? No. To me? Yes! It's not what I, Basile Duchon, deserve! He must pay . . ."

"And, if he doesn't?"

"A consequence I must consider . . ."

"Did you call her?"

"I did, but I haven't heard anything . . ."

"How long?"

Ryan checked his watch. "Hours." Quiet, he gazed out of Colbie's hotel window, thinking of the Italian patternmaker. "Of course, I don't know her well, but she didn't strike me as the type of person to ignore my texts, or calls . . ."

"Well, we can't wait any longer—Kevin and I need to get to the venue. The show opens tomorrow, and there's something I need to do . . ."

"Which is?"

"Meet with Basile . . ."

Ryan stared at her, baffled. "Didn't he make a big deal out of not contacting him during the shows?"

Colbie nodded. "He did—but, I have no doubt he hasn't been truthful with me about what we're investigating."

"You mean he lied to us?"

"Not really—I just think there's much more going on than trying to figure out who was behind his fashion career demise a few years back. It's deeper than that—he knows exactly who it is, and he hired us to simply corroborate his suspicions . . ."

"Maybe—but, it seems like an awfully expensive ruse. If he suspects anyone, why not keep us out of it? And, if that's the case, it will only serve to complicate things . . ."

"You might be right—but, I guarantee he knows damned well who's behind it."

"Coniglio?"

Colbie nodded, then took off her glasses, laying them on the table. "The more I hear his name, the more I believe his hold on the fashion industry isn't based only on design."

Ryan got up, grabbed his coat, then headed for the door. "Keep in touch—I'll let you know if I hear from Chiara."

"Madelinne, too . . ."

A darkening shadow crossed Ryan's face. "Why her?"

Colbie stared at him, wondering if she heard correctly. Was there a reason he didn't want the designer considered complicit? It wasn't, however, the time to question—both had work to do. "No reason—just keep me posted. My gut is telling me to be on guard . . ."

"From Coniglio?"

She nodded. "Or, Russo . . ."

Ryan turned the door handle. "Same thing . . ."

Giorgia Mancini lit a cigarette, flicking the gold lighter three times before it was primed to do business. "What did he want to know?

The voice on the other end crackled and faded, struggling to make the most of an unacceptable connection. "How I knew Valentine was a bogus name . . ."

A slow, deliberate drag. "Did you tell him?"

"Of course not. But, if I know Duchon, he'll not forget my words . . ."

Giorgia was silent, considering how best to handle the situation. "Have you seen her?"

"Here? In London?"

"Where else?"

"Not yet—but, I suspect our paths will cross. She seems persistent, and I won't be surprised if she seeks me out again."

"Tell me—she kept asking about Armond. Do you know why?"

"No—but, it was clear he was the focus of her attention."

"Attention? Perhaps a better word is investigation . . ."

Belle Cunningham peered through French doors leading to the garden. "What is that?" She stepped closer. "Oliver!" She waited. "Oliver! Come here!"

"Oh, for God's sake! What now? You know I'm preparing for the hunt!"

She pointed. "What . . . is that?"

Her husband stepped up to the doors, adjusting his glasses for a better look. "Good God! Is that what I think it is?"

"It looks like . . . an arm!"

"By, Jove—you're right! It's a bloody arm!"

Belle sat, her face blanching with the thought of a frozen arm resting against their lawn chair, making a mental note to have their butler toss it in the trash. Then, she looked at the dog. "It was you," she accused, pointing a finger toward its wagging tail.

"Killie?"

"Well, how else would a severed arm get in our garden, Oliver? It's not like someone visited, then left without it . . ."

"Well, my dear, someone is certainly missing it . . ."

Both were silent, none of the possibilities of how it got there, pleasant. "I suppose we should call the authorities," her husband suggested, then checked his watch. "A bloody, severed arm—this is the last thing I need!"

CHAPTER

11

Ryan switched his cell to his left ear so he could take notes. "Are you sure?"

A sniffle. "Yes—I heard from the girls in the sample room. No one's seen her since yesterday . . ."

"That doesn't mean anything's wrong—I'm sure she'll show up. Maybe she's sick, and doesn't feel like answering the phone."

"During Fashion Week? I don't think so . . ."

"Well . . . what do you think?"

"I don't know, but I have a feeling it's not good . . ."

Ryan was quiet, wondering why Madelinne chose to call him with her concerns. "Did you contact the authorities?"

"No—I feel it isn't my place. That should be left to her family . . ."

He noted Madelinne's curious phrase. "That sounds serious—do you think something's happened to her?"

A controlled silence until the fashion designer decided her call was foolish. "I don't know—but, as you said, I'm sure she'll show up!" With a promise to get in touch soon, she clicked off.

But, as hard as he tried, theirs was a conversation he couldn't erase from his mind. There was something urgent in Madelinne's voice, sounding as if she were divulging information that could get her into trouble. Deep trouble. *If that's the case,* he thought, *who's driving the bus?*

Colbie and Kevin arrived at the runway venue, its electric energy palpable as designers, models, and assistants tended to last minute, finest details. Privacy, they learned from New York, was non-existent as models changed garments within the collection, making Kevin uncomfortable as Colbie approached anyone who looked as if they might give her five seconds of their time.

"This feels so different than New York," Kevin observed as he focused his camera lens on models practicing their walk to show the garment at its best.

"I know what you mean—there's an undercurrent of something. Something unpleasant . . ."

"It's a different energy, that's for sure—not so fun."

Colbie nodded. "Agreed. It feels dark . . ."

It was clear no one was interested in speaking with them even though they represented an opportunity to provide a little press time. "It's as if they've been instructed not to talk to us," Kevin mentioned, noting glances in their direction.

"But, why? Nobody has any idea of who we are—as far as they know, we're in the biz, but on the other side of the aisle."

"Maybe . . ."

There was a concern in Kevin's voice Colbie hadn't previously heard, prompting her to wonder what was really bugging him. "Are you uncomfortable?"

"Uncomfortable? No—but, it's pretty clear getting info from anyone here is going to be like pulling teeth . . ."

A prophetic observation.

After three hours of cruising the backstage floor, Colbie realized Kevin was correct—no one was willing to talk. "Let's get out of here—we have a ritzy gig for cocktail hour, and I want to go over all of my notes beforehand. There are a few people I want to keep an eye on . . ."

"Such as?"

"Luca Russo, for one—I don't trust him as far as I can throw him." As the words left her mouth, there was no explaining the slight tinge of excitement she felt at the thought of the distinguished Italian.

"You're sure he'll be there?"

Colbie nodded. "I'm sure . . ."

"When did you first notice . . . the arm?"

Belle glanced at her husband, then turned her attention to the inspector. "Why, this morning, first thing! Oliver was preparing for the hunt and, I was . . ." She paused, her memory clearly failing her at the moment.

"You were getting ready to serve up my porridge, my dear . . ."

"Oh, yes! That's it—I walked by the window, and couldn't believe my eyes!"

Oliver nodded. "Of course, she called for me . . ."

Inspector Fallinglough scratched a few notes. "It seems the natural thing to do . . ." Another scribble. "Do you have any idea . . ."

"Who it belongs to?" Belle stood, as if preparing to leave the room in a queenie huff. "You insult my intelligence, Inspector—if I knew that, I would have let you in on it by now!"

"I meant no offense, Ma'am—but, it is strange for a perfectly good arm to wind up in your garden, propped up against a chair . . ."

"Killie dragged it in, of course . . ."

"Killie?"

Belle nodded, again taking her seat. "Our dog—well, it's Oliver's dog, really . . ."

"And, you think the dog dragged it onto your garden patio?"

"Well, how else would it have gotten there?"

Oliver glanced at the inspector. "I think that's the point of his question, my dear . . ."

The inspector nodded. "It also seems strange Killie—no matter how talented—may have a problem propping it up on the chair leg, so perfectly placed."

"Well . . ."

"Inspector," Oliver interrupted, "we really don't know anything else. My wife discovered the arm, I agreed to its particular body part, and we called you. That's the extent of it . . ."

Realizing the opportunity for gaining additional information was quickly waning, Inspector Fallinglough offered the usual. "The medical examiner will take charge of the arm, and there will be several of my men poking around."

He paused. "If you think of anything we should know, get in touch . . ." He plucked a business card from his jacket pocket. "My personal extension is on the back . . "

With that, he stepped through the French doors onto the garden patio, scanning the yard. It was, of course, possible the Cunningham's yellow lab decided to bring his newfound treasure home to share with his owners. As far as he could tell, there were no footprints and, when touching base with his officers, they concurred—it seemed to show up out of nowhere.

At least we can get fingerprints, the inspector thought, watching as the medical examiner carefully positioned the arm in a plastic bag, then in a cooler.

I hope . . .

The frigid winter day stepped aside for an early evening as Colbie stared at herself in the bathroom mirror. Although life had been kind, traces of it were beginning to show— along with a familiar doubt surfacing only when she realized she should have done something differently. *Kara Vaughan wasn't even on my radar,* she thought as she applied delicate eyeliner, then mascara. *How could I have been so dense?*

An important question.

The tug of her shadow world made itself known as she slipped into a trendy cocktail dress, then checked her hair one more time before heading for the elevator. As much as she hated to admit it, retreating to a place of comfort was compelling—still, she knew she could do no such thing.

Kevin whistled as she turned the corner. "Is is rude to whistle at my partner," he asked, grinning.

"Maybe in some circles, but not mine!" She laughed, pushing the elevator button. "I appreciate the compliment!"

Moments later, they stood at the hotel's curb, watching as the driver Basile commissioned for them pulled close. "Let's keep our conversation to a minimum," Colbie suggested as the chauffeur opened the passenger's door. "I'm not certain who we can trust . . ."

Within the half hour, they stepped across the threshold of a ritzy pad in Notting Hill, playground for the rich and famous. As they entered the lavish penthouse, Colbie noticed designer elites holding fragile champagne glasses with perfectly manicured fingertips, all the while keeping track of who was paying attention—a glance here or there was a game played only by the best.

"Keep your photo eye on Russo," Colbie suggested. "He's standing by the window . . ."

Kevin nodded. "Got him—do you know who he's talking to?"

Colbie plucked a champagne glass from the server's silver tray as he made the rounds. "No—I've never seen her before." Just as she was about to make her way toward him, she noticed his glance in her direction.

Moments later, he approached. "I believe we met in New York," he greeted, kissing her hand.

She smiled. "Indeed, we did—at a similar event!"

He assessed her head-to-toe look, unashamed of his obvious appreciation. "You look stunning . . ."

"You're too kind . . ." She paused. "We didn't have much of an opportunity to chat the last time we were together—how about if we find somewhere a bit more private? I have Armond on my schedule for the last day of the show, and I'd love to pick your brain . . ."

"About?"

"Oh, you know—what I need to know before I walk into the lion's den."

"The lion's den? You make him sound like a tyrant!"

Colbie coyly took his arm, guiding him to a vintage, expensive love seat in the corner of the room. "Good heavens, no! I've never met him, but I certainly don't want to look like an idiot!" She paused as she sat, then patted the seat beside her. "So, Mr. Russo—is there anything I should know?"

Luca hesitated, then sat beside her, the thought of enjoying her company titillating. "I can tell you little—but, I assure you, he's not the man you hear of in the press."

"We always seem to magnify situations to their absolute worst, don't we?"

Russo took a sip of champagne, then turned his complete attention to the beautiful redhead. "I trust you'll have the good sense not to do so . . ."

Is that a warning? Colbie didn't take her eyes from his. "Precisely the reason I want to talk to you . . ." She paused. "What's he like?"

"Armond? Enormously talented . . ."

Colbie nodded. "I agree—his designs are always cutting edge. But, I'm curious about what he's like away from the runway . . ." She placed her hand on his. "I won't use any of our conversation. It's totally off the record . . ." Then, she, too, sipped her champagne, allowing him a few moments to decide if he wanted to spend more time with her.

"Perhaps," he offered, allowing her hand to linger, "we should have this discussion at a different time—a different place."

"A good idea," Colbie agreed. "Where do you suggest?"

Kevin watched from across the room, his lens surreptitiously capturing moments of their conversation. *What are you up to, Colbie,* he wondered, noticing her mannerisms change almost imperceptibly.

Although Colbie knew he was snapping pics, she managed to keep Luca Russo's attention on her, rather than on other guests. "And, when?"

He gave her hand a slight squeeze, then stood. "I'll be in touch . . ."

"I beg your forgiveness for scheduling our meeting so early," Basile commented as he ushered Colbie to his temporary, London living quarters. As much as he enjoyed designing, Fashion Week shows in four countries made it impossible to maintain living his life under the radar, something causing considerable consternation.

"No apology necessary . . ." She sat in the chair of his choice, waiting until he made himself comfortable. "I'm guessing you're wondering why I need to see you . . ."

"Oui—it is my recollection we decided not to meet until after the conclusion of all events."

Colbie nodded. "Of course, you're correct—however, it's come to my attention there may be . . . elements . . . of our agreement causing question."

"And, it's come to my attention, Ms. Colleen, your approach to those within my circle was less than subtle. Your true identity was readily discovered—something I find greatly disappointing."

"I'm not aware of . . ."

"I know you're not, Ms. Colleen—and, that's an issue with which I take considerable exception."

Colbie's face flushed—it had been a long time since anyone called her out for her actions. "Did you not think it was necessary to inform me as to who is in your employ?"

Duchon smiled. "Ah—you must be speaking of Kara Vaughan. My marketing director . . ."

Colbie listened, noting a coolness in her client's voice, unlike when they first met in Paris. "Yes . . . and, it makes me curious, Basile—whom else don't I know?"

Duchon said nothing, assessing whether he made an egregious error when bringing Colbie Colleen into the mix. There was something about her he found disquieting despite her international reputation. "It is not necessary for you to contact those in my employ. In fact, I'd rather you didn't— you were hired specifically to infiltrate Armond Coniglio's design house, and it seems you have accomplished little."

"I don't think . . ."

"Exactly. I question my decision to hire you, Ms. Colleen. It's as simple as that . . ."

Colbie's face set, realizing the conversation turned without her having an ounce of control. In that moment, she knew she had to force his hand. "Do you prefer we sever our agreement?"

Silence. Then, a sigh. "No . . ." A sustained pause. "Perhaps, I made a mistake by not telling you of Kara Vaughan. As you probably figured out, it was my calculated maneuver—I should have anticipated your connecting with her during the investigation."

"Perhaps, you should have . . ."

Then, as she watched, Basile Duchon's resolve dissolved, leaving her to witness a man whose life was out of control.

A broken man.

CHAPTER

12

Giorgia eyed the model, appreciating her ability to shake off gossip and years as if they were nothing. Since her orchestrated fall from grace a few years back, many surmised a successful return would be impossible—and, for a while, it seemed they were correct. But, without warning, she resurfaced, rising to acclaim no one expected. Was such fame in the industry warranted? Perhaps. Although, there were those who were displeased with her return.

"I had the opportunity to speak with Kara . . ."

Marguerite arranged her coat around her shoulders. "And . . ."

"It is obvious we must be careful—as we suspected, Basile hired Colbie Colleen."

"Ah, yes—Valentine. From what I understand, she's tenacious . . ."

Giorgia leaned back in the bistro booth with a window, her eye catching someone on the street. She watched for a moment, then returned her attention to the model. "We knew that—but, her attention is squarely on Armond, and we can't let her disrupt our plan."

Marguerite smiled slightly, as if amused by a private joke. "Perhaps I should have told you—I had a bit of fun with Ms. Colleen."

"Fun? I'm not sure I like the sound of that . . ."

"It was harmless, really—but, I simply couldn't help myself."

"Do you care to share?"

"It is of no consequence . . ." Marguerite, too, focused on the street, speaking to Giorgia without offering the courtesy of looking her in the eye. "Armond is beginning to suspect—what, I'm not sure."

"Why do you think that?"

"Innuendo and rumor circulating through our London circles . . ."

"Regarding?"

"His actions—and, lack of integrity." Marguerite Villanova returned her attention to Giorgia. "My instinct tells me things are about to change—and, Armond Coniglio is at the center of it."

"Excellent! Our position couldn't be more perfect . . ."

News of Chiara's grisly demise hit the wires on London Fashion Week's opening day, few seeming to notice, or care. After all, she wasn't an integral part of the shows with only a handful knowing her name. But, those few who did know her, mourned her passing—for a minute or two.

All in all, the first day of runway shows went off without issues, Colbie and Kevin not hearing the news about Chiara until Ryan filled them in late that evening. "Madelinne's gut feeling was correct," he commented, as the three of them made themselves comfortable in Colbie's suite. "It was clear she was pretty upset when she called me . . ."

"But, why? Why would anyone want to take out someone like Chiara? From what you said earlier, she was a nice, young lady . . ." Kevin glanced at Ryan, then Colbie. Getting an up close and personal look at what could happen to turn an investigation sideways was intimidating, especially when things morphed into murder.

"That's the question, isn't it?" Colbie turned her attention to Ryan. "What do you think? You're the one who's had contact with her . . ."

"I wish I had an answer . . ."

Colbie kicked off her shoes. "Have you talked to Madelinne since it happened?"

"No—I'm waiting to see if she's going to call me. I'll be surprised if she doesn't have some idea about it, but I don't know if she'll talk . . ."

"Well, I think you should reach out. Are you comfortable with calling her for another evening drink?"

"Of course—I don't want it to be perceived as poor taste, however."

"From what you told me about her, I doubt it will be. Besides, she called you about Chiara before we knew she was murdered. You have the perfect reason to get in touch with her . . ."

Ryan nodded. "You're right. I'll call . . ."

"I trust everything is in order—I heard the news."

"You doubt my ability to perform?"

Armond Coniglio eyed the first look in his fashion collection, eager to be in the limelight once again. "No— but, it is always wise to follow up. What concerns me is how quickly authorities identified the body . . ." He turned to Russo, a hard glint in his eyes. "An error, don't you agree?"

"I assume you're speaking of the arm found on an estate outside of the city . . ."

"Indeed. Perhaps you should explain . . ."

"There's little to explain. It was an unavoidable circumstance . . ."

"Few things are unavoidable . . ."

"Well, this was—my decision to scatter her was excellent. What I didn't expect, however, was her right arm tumbling down the embankment into the frigid water, its placement completely rendering it inaccessible." Russo paused, recalling the gruesome scene. "Recovering it was impossible . . ."

"Clearly, it wasn't that inaccessible—otherwise it wouldn't have wound up propped against a garden chair."

The hair at the back of Russo's neck bristled. He wasn't accustomed to having his methods questioned, and it was a slight against his professionalism he didn't appreciate. "I have no idea how it got there, I assure you. Perhaps the current carried it . . ."

Armond turned to him, his face refusing to disguise obvious disdain. As far as he was concerned, his directive was simple—one that should not have secured authorities' attention. Surely, now that the damage was done, there would be questions—a position he didn't relish.

As he considered the issue, he also considered—again— if it were time to make changes within his organization. Disappointment in his right-hand man was becoming familiar, prompting him to wonder if Luca Russo could be trusted to perform his duties without babysitting. "Current, or no current—the result is the same. It is a mistake that can cost us everything!"

In that moment, Armond Coniglio made a decision.

It was, indeed, time for a change . . .

CHAPTER

13

*M*uch of their time was spent trying to snag interviews, but, as much as Colbie didn't understand it, there was no question Kevin's initial observation was correct.

Nothing, but the cold shoulder.

Days two and three at London Fashion Week offered little in the way of additional information—a situation she found intolerable. "Someone," she commented to Ryan and Kevin as they enjoyed a merlot nightcap, "put the kibosh on talking to us. So, we need to figure out who it is, pronto. Something like this? It can kill our investigation . . ."

"Not only for London, but Milan and Paris, too . . ." Kevin handed her his tablet. "Check it out . . ."

"What is it?" Ryan leaned forward for a better view.

"Backstage footage of yesterday's show—but, I'm not going to tell you anything. See for yourself—I edited it without sound because it was nothing but unintelligible conversation. There was too much backstage noise . . ."

"You kept the original?" Colbie scooted closer to Ryan, then tapped the screen.

"Of course . . ."

Both watched as models, designers, and assistants scrambled to prepare for their walks, most of Kevin's footage of the main runway's backstage. "Wait! Who's that?" Colbie watched for several more seconds, then stopped the video.

Ryan leaned closer. "I have no idea—and, it's someone not on our radar. No photos of this guy anywhere in our notes . . ."

"Well, whoever he is, he seems to be buddy-buddy with Armond Coniglio."

"And, it's pretty clear they're not having a pleasant conversation. In fact, Coniglio looks downright pissed . . ."

"You ain't seen nothin' yet . . . " Kevin eyed both of them. "Keep watching . . ."

Two minutes and fifteen seconds later, Colbie sat back on the couch. "Holy crap! I wish I could hear what they were saying . . ."

Her newest partner nodded. "I know—and, the original isn't any better. That's why I edited it without sound—it was more of a pain in the ass, than anything."

"Judging from the couple of minutes Kevin captured their conversation, I'll bet the farm they aren't friends. That was way more than two friends not seeing eye to eye—the other guy looked as if he were about to blow."

Colbie nodded. "Agreed—but, no matter how you cut it, this guy is a new player. Unfortunately, there's no way to find out who he is—I can't start asking questions without causing more suspicion."

"The good news is," Kevin offered, "we have him on camera. It won't be difficult to find him on the Internet if he has any kind of presence, at all . . ."

"If he doesn't?"

"Then . . ."

Colbie propped her feet up on the coffee table. "We start digging . . ."

Ryan was quiet for a moment. "You're seeing Coniglio tomorrow, right?"

"Yes . . ."

"What do you think about steering the conversation toward what we just watched?"

Colbie closed her eyes, taking time to respond. Finally, she focused on both of them. "It's a start . . ."

Ryan agreed. "I think so, too—but, I'm beginning to wonder if there's something about Armond Coniglio we know nothing about . . ."

"Such as?"

"Well—it's clear the guy he was talking to wasn't the Ward Cleaver type. I wouldn't want to meet that guy in a well-lit alley, let alone a dark one . . ."

"How about," Kevin suggested, "we don't get ahead of ourselves. Let me work on it, and I'll have something . . ."

"If there is anything," Colbie interrupted.

"Right—if there's something I think you should look at, I'll let you know." He checked his watch. "So—that means I'm going to have a late night . . ." With that, he was up, heading toward the door. "You'll know by seven . . ."

By six-thirty, Colbie was showered and dressed, her thoughts consumed by the argument between Armond Coniglio, and the unknown man. As much as she would have liked to tap into her intuition, when she tried, there was little.

Fifteen minutes later, Kevin was at her door.

"I take it you have news," she greeted, an empty coffee cup in her hand. "Want some?"

"Hell, yes! If I don't get caffeine in me, I'm going to be worthless today!"

"How late were you up?"

"Until three—finally, I couldn't keep my eyes open, so I called it a night."

"Good work! Go ahead and make yourself comfortable while I pour . . ."

Minutes later and after a few slow sips of nature's alarm clock, Kevin filled her in. "Giuseppe Marino—a wannabe top rung family member."

"Family, as in mob?"

"One and the same—but, Marino didn't make the cut. According to newspaper reports within the last several years, he was picked up on a few different charges, none of which seemed to stick. A memorable résumé when trying to impress your soon-to-be boss . . ."

"He probably had a good lawyer—but, what does he have to do with Armond Coniglio?"

"Good question—I don't know much, but it's not difficult to figure they're more than acquaintances, judging by the video."

"I agree . . ." Colbie was quiet, thinking about her two o'clock appointment with the designer. "At least I have a name . . ."

"I'm glad you called . . ."

"To be honest, I wasn't sure if I should—when I heard the news about Chiara, I didn't want to intrude."

Madelinne shook her head. "I can't believe it—why would anyone want to kill her?"

Ryan reached across the table, taking her hand. "That's what we need to find out . . ." For the first time as an criminal investigator, Ryan felt a tug of duplicity—as much as he would have liked to tell Madelinne about the investigation, there was nothing in him to make him cross the line.

"How? Besides, City of London Police are on it, and it's only a matter of time until the Yard is called in . . ."

"They're probably already involved—I can't imagine they aren't. Body parts found on a ritzy estate certainly qualifies . . ."

Madelinne's eyes filled with tears. "I couldn't believe it when I heard—poor Chiara!"

"I agree—so, let's try to sort it out. Do you have time?"

She nodded. "I'll make time—how about if we order lunch?"

"Good idea . . ."

Minutes later, their orders were with the server, leaving time for confidential conversation. "I didn't tell you," Madelinne continued, "but, Chiara and I were dear friends, although Armond frowned on my fraternizing with anyone in the sample room . . ."

"Even though you managed his operation?"

"He meant on a personal level—being friends with the help was something he wouldn't tolerate."

"Why? That doesn't make sense! Isn't it better to have a positive work atmosphere?"

"One would think—but, Armond Coniglio is a man who believes in class levels. Anyone associated with him, directly, is expected to maintain a certain decorum . . ."

"You mean one of snobbery . . ."

"Well, yes. As sad as that is . . ."

Ryan was quiet, wondering if he should ask the question he needed answered. "Do you mind if I ask you a personal question?"

"That depends . . ."

"On?"

"How personal . . ."

Again, he was quiet. "It's pretty personal . . ." He watched intently as she decided whether she could trust him.

"Go ahead—ask."

"Okay—was your relationship with Armond Coniglio personal, too?"

She looked him square in the eye. "Yes. Does that make a difference?"

"In what way?"

"To you . . ."

Ryan wasn't quite sure what to say. He had to admit, he enjoyed her company—and, it had been a long time since he had anyone in his life. "Well . . ." He blushed, hoping she didn't see.

She did. "I'm sorry—I didn't mean to embarrass you!"

"Does it show?"

She laughed. "Just a little—I apologize for being so blunt."

"That's okay! Blunt is good—but, how about if we table that part of our conversation for another time? Right now, we need to concentrate on who murdered Chiara . . ."

Madelinne nodded, enjoying the few moments of normalcy—it had been a long time since being with someone so intriguing. "You're right . . ."

For their remaining time together, she recounted how she and Chiara became friends, although strictly forbidden by Armond Coniglio, as well as details of her relationship with him. Personal details.

Unpleasant details.

By the time they walked out the pub's door, neither quite knew what to say. But, one thing was clear . . .

They connected.

"I trust you're prepared . . ."

Armond Coniglio stood in front of his suite's foyer mirror, straightening his tie. "Prepared for what? A fifteen minute interview with a reporter?" His questions were, of course, rhetorical. "Such a conversation takes no preparation—agreed?"

Luca Russo studied the man in front of the mirror, realizing and giving credence to his creeping dislike. There was no doubt their relationship was strained, although he wasn't sure why—even so, being on Armond's bad side was a position he didn't relish.

"I'm sure you know best, Armond—but, what do you know of her? Valentine . . ."

"I know she has one name—I think that is enough. I also know her fifteen minutes with me will be fifteen of the greatest moments of her life . . ." He stood back, admiring his reflection. "Don't you agree?"

"Perhaps . . ."

Even though Russo spent time with her at the Notting Hill cocktail party, he hadn't acted on his invitation to meet her at another time, and place. The truth was he was still considering what it was about her he didn't trust. Beauty aside, there was something about her nudging him to be wary, and he felt it was his duty to pass his thoughts on to his boss. *But, if you're too foolish to listen, Armond—you deserve what you get . . .*

CHAPTER

14

Oscar Hallberg kept his eyes glued to the television, listening to every word as the British reporter recounted the Cunningham's astonishment at finding an arm on their terrace. "It was absolutely ghastly," Belle told him. "I'm not sure I'll ever be the same . . ."

Oliver hastily assured her she would be fine, then excused themselves—having Belle in the spotlight wasn't a particularly good idea.

Finally, as the station cut to commercial, Hallberg realized things just got a whole lot trickier. There was a new feeling of urgency as he considered possible changes—but, thinking through achievements, doing something rash because of a renegade arm didn't make sense.

It did raise his antennae, however. Since his conversation with Basile Duchon, there was no doubt something was afoot—what, he didn't know. Not only that, there seemed to be a new player—one causing those who normally didn't look twice to keep a wary eye on their surroundings, as well as who was talking to who. It was an undercurrent, really—one that had the stench of Armond Coniglio all over it.

Picking up his cell, he carefully weighed his options. *If I change plans now, will it be worth it? My position is already precarious merely by my presence . . .*

Finally, a decision. Tapping his cell screen, he waited as the home screen's gallery of his designs bloomed to life. Another tap. One ring. Two. Then, three.

No connection.

It's not like you to ignore my calls, he thought, placing his cell on the end table. *I can only hope there is an acceptable reason . . .*

Although her interview was at two o'clock, Colbie arrived fifteen minutes early, providing enough time to shed the energy of the runway. Winter's sun already started to turn, prompting her to choose a stately chair by a floor-to-ceiling window. The rays' waning warmth felt marvelous as she closed her eyes, clearing her mind of everything except her interview with Armond Coniglio.

Even with all of her research, pangs of uncertainty clutched her stomach. Conversations with insiders indicated a man capable of many things and, as she sat, she knew there was much more to him than being only a designer. Kevin dug into his past, but doing so revealed little—Coniglio was squeaky clean, excluding articles touting his disagreement with Basile Duchon. *We know Basile wants to take you down for ruining his career,* she thought, *but, what don't I know?*

Just then, her watch alarm sounded.

It was time.

Minutes later, she stepped off the elevator, Luca Russo waiting to greet her. "Ms. Valentine—how nice to see you." His tone was cool—nothing like when she spoke to him at the cocktail party.

Colbie extended her hand. "Mr. Russo—thank you. I appreciate Mr. Coniglio's time . . ."

"I'm afraid, however, your time will be short . . ."

Just what Colbie didn't want to hear. "I'm sorry to hear that, but I'm looking forward to it." She paused. "How long do we have? I'll tailor my questions to fit his schedule . . ."

"Fifteen minutes . . ."

"Oh . . . my!"

Russo excused himself, reappearing moments later with the world's most important fashion designer of the time. "Armond, please meet Valentine . . ."

Colbie stood, although seconds later she wondered why. "Mr. Coniglio—thank you for taking time to meet with me. Much appreciated . . ."

He didn't offer his hand. "Yes, yes—please sit." He waited. "I'm afraid we don't have long . . ."

In that moment, Colbie decided her abbreviated time with him would offer little in the way of usable information. So, she had two choices—ask questions of no consequence, or jump in the deep end. "I'll try to be as succinct as possible. First, please accept my condolences regarding Chiara . . ." She watched him carefully, noting subtle facial and body shifts. Nothing. "Do you believe her murder has anything to do with you?"

Coniglio's eyebrows arched, a slight twitch tugging at the corner of his mouth. "Me? Why would her unfortunate passing have anything to do with me?"

"Well—it stands to reason, doesn't it, someone might be targeting you?"

He smiled. "You have quite a vivid imagination, Ms. Valentine. But, I assure you, Chiara Ricci's murder has nothing to do with me. I mourn her passing, as does everyone within my organization . . ."

"Why do you think she was murdered?" Again, she kept her attention on every response. Every move.

"I don't have any idea . . ." He stood, indicating their interview was over. "Now, if you'll please excuse me . . ."

Luca appeared from nowhere, cuing Colbie he listened to their conversation, waiting for Armond to cut it short—as always.

She, too, stood, offering her hand. "Thank you for your time . . ."

A gesture he refused to accept.

"Luca will see you out."

Colbie watched as he disappeared into what she could only surmise was a bedroom. "You're right, Mr. Russo," she commented, turning to him. "What an interesting man . . ."

"Indeed—I hope he answered all of your questions."

"Oh, yes!" She paused, smiling. "He gave me everything I needed . . ."

By the close of London Fashion Week, there was little doubt Armond Coniglio was involved in something he preferred to keep private. *Then again*, Colbie thought, *so is Basile Duchon* . . .

It was a thought prompting a final, London late-night conversation. "I think we need to shift our focus from the runways," she suggested as they met for a debrief after the event's last door was locked. "My gut is telling me everything rests with Armond Coniglio, and Basile Duchon."

Ryan glanced at Kevin. "But, we knew that already . . ."

"I know—but, I feel as if something's shifting, and we're being led in a completely new direction."

"Okay—so, we focus only on those two. Anything else?"

"Yes—there's someone else involved. Someone running under the radar . . ."

"Do you know who," Kevin asked, "and, for what reason?"

She thought for a moment. "Who? I don't know. Why? Total ruination . . ."

Giuseppe Marino was in a tricky position, as he knew he would be when accepting a job with his new employer—but, the truth was his allegiance was with whomever paid him what he was worth. Always motivated by the almighty dollar, there wasn't much he wouldn't do to feel its comfort in his hands—and, it was a view of life for which he held no regret. Or, apology.

But, dissent and dissatisfaction with one who was an old friend? An uncomfortable situation. He and Armond Coniglio formed a childhood bond, one both thought impervious to tests of time—but, as often happens, their friendship was as breakable as anyone else's. The conversation backstage sent both to their corners, licking their wounds, each knowing he would come out on top.

The untenable bond of arrogance.

Yet, it was odd the way it went down. As a confidant for his new employer, Marino's first assignment was to keep an eye on everything Coniglio—where he went, who he was with, and for how long. Not only Armond, but Luca Russo, as well—so, when he tailed him to a river outside of London at the beginning of the week, he was full witness to actions involving Coniglio's gal from the sample room. It wasn't a stretch to figure chucking body parts into the river would be frowned upon by London's finest—and, letting his childhood friend know he could keep his mouth shut—well, it was the perfect way to make a few extra bucks.

That knowledge, however, put him in an interesting position—report what he saw to his new employer? Probably the best approach. Unfortunately, it wasn't the path to a fatter wallet. Still, if he saw Russo pitch the arm into the river, others could have, too. Wasn't it his duty to warn his childhood friend? One would think—but, when Marino told Armond he knew about Luca Russo's nefarious activities, it was a complete shock when Coniglio didn't want to hear any of it. He exploded, dissolving their friendship, as well as any working alliances they may have forged.

Giuseppe's last conversation with Armond backstage at London Fashion Week left a bad taste in his mouth, and it was only by the grace of God no one witnessed it. Not one of his most professional moments, he agreed—but, what was one to do when confronted with a bout of conscience?

Still, he took a chance.

Backfired.

Although Chiara's murder was technically none of Colbie's business, she couldn't get it out of her mind, certain Armond Coniglio was at the crux of it—his reaction to her bringing it up during the interview was interesting, and it was clear he didn't want to talk.

"Let's continue with our plan," she suggested to Ryan and Kevin as they disembarked their Milan flight. "We'll still play our parts, but most of our work will be outside of the Fashion Week venues . . ."

Ryan agreed. "I'm on Coniglio surveillance, and Kevin can spell me so I can get some rest . . ."

"Perfect—and, I booked us into different hotels. I don't want anyone getting hip to the fact you work with me—they expect Kevin, but not you." She glanced at Kevin who was navigating their way to baggage claim. "Your hotel is only a couple of blocks from mine . . ."

Within the hour, Duchon's Milan driver picked them up, first dropping Colbie at her hotel, then Ryan and Kevin. After the rush of packing, reporting to Basile, and making plans for a more targeted investigation, she welcomed the quiet of her room, wasting no time to unpack, take a shower, then curl up in her bathrobe on the couch.

As she relaxed, thoughts turned to London. Armond. Chiara. *According to Ryan,* she recalled, *Chiara wasn't exactly singing Coniglio's praises—and, with an ego like his, I'm guessing he wouldn't take it well.*

Sitting in the glow of soft lamplight, she allowed her intuitive mind to leap to life, hoping for information on Armond Coniglio—instead, she saw nothing, but a figure. As she watched, it clasped hands with someone—who, Colbie couldn't see. *It's definitely male,* she thought, making her wonder about the designer's relationships.

Making a mental note to ask Ryan, a different image began to form—again, a shadowed figure, but it was different from the vision she had a few weeks earlier. She watched as it crumpled to the ground, hand outstretched, begging her help. As the vision took hold, the image sharpened, and she began to recognize its form.

Madelinne!

Prior to arriving in Milan, Colbie, Ryan, and Kevin decided to take a day to relax—the pace of the fashion shows was staggering, and all three were running on empty. Of course, they communicated, but, as far as their time?

Theirs for whatever they wanted to do.

"You ready?" Ryan checked his watch. "Where do you want to meet?"

A short conversation later, plans were solidified, both promising not to be late.

Precisely at two, he pulled on the restaurant door, breaking into a smile as Madelinne greeted him. "You're prompt! I like that in a man . . ."

"A habit from childhood," he laughed as he caught the hostess's eye.

A couple of minutes later, they were seated at a table for two close to the bar. "Perfect," Madelinne laughed, "but, I'm limiting my intake to one glass of wine!"

"Did you have lunch?"

"No, and, I'm starving . . ."

After deciding on an appetizer and placing their order with the server, both were quiet, neither sure of what to say. "So," Ryan began, "I see you escaped London, unscathed . . ."

She nodded. "Barely—you know, in all of my years in this business . . ." Her voice trailed as she thought of her friend. "I never thought I'd see anything like last week . . ."

"I know—how are you doing?"

She took a sip of chardonnay. "I'm okay—the Yard doesn't have anything yet."

Ryan shook his head. "You don't know that—we don't have any idea of the evidence they've accumulated so far . . ."

She cocked her head, looking at him. "You sound like a cop . . ."

In that moment, Ryan knew to pull back, unwilling to break his cover. If Madelinne found out he was part of an investigative firm, chances of her never seeing him again were pretty good—and, if she found out he was Colbie's partner?

So much for inside information.

"Too many cop shows," he admitted, grinning. "But, you have to agree it makes sense because the investigation is just beginning . . ." He paused. "What do you think?"

"About?"

"Who killed Chiara . . ." He waited, wondering if she would take him into her confidence.

Madelinne was quiet as she thought of who had the most to gain. "When I was in London, I heard talk . . ."

"From whom?"

"A few people . . ."

Ryan didn't say anything, knowing she was struggling with telling him what she considered to be the truth. "About," he prompted.

"Armond . . ."

"Do you think he's responsible for Chiara's murder?"

Madelinne nodded. "I'm certain of it . . ."

"I don't know—Coniglio doesn't strike me as the type of guy who would murder someone on the outskirts of town in the middle of winter. Let alone carve up the body—besides, why would he?"

"You don't know Armond—he's a proud, arrogant man. Chiara mentioned more than once she thought he was as dirty as the day is long."

"Did she ever say why she thought that?"

"Not directly. But, she did say she thought he was a fraud . . ."

"A fraud? You mean the designs aren't his?" Ryan held his breath slightly, waiting for her answer.

"No—he designs everything. I know that to be fact . . ."

Ryan shook his head. "Then, I don't understand . . ."

"Neither do I—but, like I said, she mentioned it several times. Not just to me, but to others in the sample room, as well . . ."

"Maybe she mentioned it one time too many . . ."

"Precisely—there's no doubt in my mind he's capable of it." She paused. "You're right, though—Armond would never do such dirty work himself. That's why he passes every deed to Luca Russo . . ."

Ryan sat back in his chair, not taking his eyes from her. "Do you know that because of your personal relationship with Coniglio?"

"Yes—after my first year with him, it was clear he was ruthless and cunning. And, dangerous . . ."

"You know that, first hand?"

Madelinne nodded. "My relationship with him was one of abuse—and, he treated his models the same way."

"Are you referring to physical abuse?"

"Yes—but, only with me. He threatened models with ruining their careers if they chose to go against his wishes.

They were never to question what they were wearing, or the garments' fabric. Such talk was strictly forbidden . . ."

"Why did the models put up with it?"

"Because Armond was right—he could ruin anyone's career by snapping his fingers. If you don't believe me, ask Marguerite Villanova . . ."

"I thought the split between her and Duchon had something to do with a disagreement between them . . ."

"Oh, no—every bit of it was orchestrated by Armond. I heard there was a movement to take him down, but nothing ever came of it."

"What do you mean? Who tried to take him down?"

"Oh, I don't think the plan got very far—I heard rumblings a few months ago. From what I can tell, nothing happened—but, if he heard? Well, let's just say he wouldn't put up with it . . ."

"Which is why you think he had something to do with Chiara . . ."

"Yes! But, what I think doesn't count. I can't take my suspicion to the Yard . . ."

"Well—yes, you can. It's the kind of information they need . . ."

Again, she cocked her head. "Are you sure you're not a cop?"

Ryan grinned. "Pretty sure . . ."

CHAPTER

15

At some point in an investigation, there comes the time when tables turn. As Luca Russo waited across the street for Colbie to depart her hotel, he couldn't help but feel a pang of disappointment. Their first meeting in New York piqued his interest, as did their second in London—in Milan?

She was one he couldn't trust.

After her meeting with Armond, he was more convinced of her duplicity—what it was, he couldn't quite figure out. There was talk of Valentine throughout the ranks, but, thus far, it was only from a press perspective. He suspected there was more, so, without blessing from his boss, he sat in a coffee shop across the street, watching the hotel's front doors.

But, by three o'clock, nothing. *Perhaps I'm being a fool,* he thought as he paid his bill, then stepped onto the sidewalk. Still, even with thoughts of foolishness, he couldn't tamp down what—in his gut—he knew to be true.

Armond Coniglio may have met his match.

"Where do you go from here," Ryan asked as Madelinne polished off her dessert.

"What do you mean? After I leave here?"

He shook his head. "No—I mean your thoughts about Armond Coniglio's being involved in Chiara's murder. Are you going to talk to the cops?"

Placing her fork on the plate, then pushing it slightly away, she looked at Ryan, stunned. "What? Are you kidding? I'm not opening my mouth! It's a good way to wind up like Chiara . . ."

"Good point. So? What now?"

"I keep doing the same old, same old—I don't want to arouse any suspicion. But . . ." She paused. "That doesn't mean I'm not going to keep my eyes open . . ."

Ryan drained the last of his water. "Probably the best plan . . ." For some reason he was feeling awkward, like the time he wanted to ask Cindy Barker on a second date when he was a junior in high school—he was pretty sure he was sweating then, too. "Will you let me know if you notice, or find something?"

"Of course—but, if I don't find anything?"

"Then . . ."

She laughed and stood, placing her napkin on the table. "You're blushing . . ."

An inarguable observation.

Her eyes met his. "I find you intriguing . . ." She purposely said nothing, waiting for his response.

"I'm not sure what to say . . ." Ryan, too, rose, then guided her to the front of the restaurant, his hand resting lightly on the small of her back.

As they stepped into the sunlight, she turned, kissing him lightly on the cheek. "I'll be in touch . . ."

He watched as she walked down the street, then turned the corner. *Am I playing with fire*, he wondered, as she disappeared.

He turned, heading the opposite direction.

Maybe . . .

A day to relax was exactly what Colbie needed and, by dinnertime, her batteries were recharged, and she was ready to move forward. On the first day of the Milan show, she'd make an appearance with Kevin, then ease on down the road to places she was sure those visiting the Italian city wouldn't go.

"You're out of your mind," Ryan told her as they munched on snacks he picked up before their meeting. "You won't like 'em and, I'm telling you, it's not safe . . ."

Although she appreciated his concern, she was growing weary of the safety mantra. "I'll be fine! Stop worrying!"

"Yeah, right—like that will ever happen!" He glanced at her, noticing a smidge of irritation creeping into her voice. Time to change the subject. "I met with Madelinne today for lunch . . ."

"Really? I didn't know . . ."

"No sense bothering you . . ."

"Bothering me?"

"Well, yes—you haven't taken any time off since we began this investigation. It's not healthy! So, I didn't want to bug you . . ."

Colbie was quiet, enjoying he was thinking of her well being. "Still . . ."

"Still, nothing—so, do you want to hear, or not?"

"Of course, I want to hear!"

Ryan grinned, then reached for a slice of Italian cheese. "I thought so . . ."

For the next hour, they discussed Ryan's lunch meeting with Madelinne, sharing the suspicion Armond Coniglio was up to his eyeballs in Chiara's murder—even so, they agreed there was nothing they could do. "I agree with Madelinne," Colbie commented as she sipped a glass of merlot, "it's becoming a far too dangerous situation."

"Precisely why I don't like your traipsing off on your own!"

She was quiet, knowing he was right. "I know," she finally admitted. "And, I think you're right—but, if someone sees you with me, there goes our cover."

"True—so, what's the solution?"

"Kevin."

"Kevin? He's as scrawny as a fencepost!"

"Yes, but he's a scrawny black belt . . ."

Ryan was silent, his brain trying to wrap around that bit of news. "Kevin's a black belt? How do you know?"

"He told me in London—he tested for it when he was just out of high school."

"Holy shit . . ."

"Yep—my guess is scrawny Kevin can take care of himself!"

"Well, I'm not worried about Kevin. I'm worried about you . . ."

Colbie smiled, knowing his concern was rooted in deep friendship. "I know—I appreciate it."

It was a tone Ryan recognized instantly—and, he knew he wasn't going to win. "Just be sure Kevin has you in his sight at all times . . ."

The first day of the show was as frenetic as the others, Colbie and Kevin making an appearance, then ducking out shortly before the evening's main runway was under the lights. Colbie's research the previous day led her to wanting to check out back street pubs and bars out of the way from tourists' naïve eyes. "I'm not really interested in the obvious," Colbie mentioned as they turned down an alley leading to a few shops, and restaurants.

"Are you looking for any place in particular?"

Colbie stopped, looking at him. "I'm guessing you already know the answer to that," she teased. "Of course!"

"Care to clue me in?"

"Okay—when I was doing my research on our day off, I began thinking about what kind of person Armond Coniglio is—and, after meeting with him, I feel he's not the type to frequent five-star restaurants."

"Makes sense—in fact, I don't recall seeing any photos of him in any sort of restaurant. So, I take it we're looking for a place that's off the beaten path . . ."

"Precisely . . ." As shadows lengthened, casting an eerie glow on a small, vintage, rock-faced tavern, she pointed to the end of the street. Within minutes, they crossed the threshold, the interior's intimate, medieval decor offering a sense of intimacy. Secrets. Illusion. Wood tables were softly illuminated with candlelight, a massive stone arch lending to its historical authenticity.

Colbie spied a table in the corner. "I guess it's a seat ourselves thing," she commented, scanning the room for a hostess.

"This place feels like locals come here—you know, the type of person who knows exactly what to expect."

"I agree. Let's head for that one . . ." She grabbed two menus from a small box affixed to the wall, then led the way, taking note of faces, as well as the general layout. Moments later, an aging waiter approached, greeting them in Italian.

"Do you speak English," Colbie asked in his native tongue—one of several, must-know phrases she learned before the case officially began.

The waiter nodded, and smiled. "I sure do!"

Fifteen minutes later, he placed two, heaping plates of spaghetti and meatballs in front of them. "Enjoy!"

"It looks wonderful," Colbie gushed, perhaps a little too much—but, she had work to do, so it made sense to be on the waiter's good side. "This is such a fabulous place—do you know the history?"

The waiter nodded. "This building is over one hundred and fifty years old, he explained. "It's said to be the meeting place for the Italian mafia when it was in its prime!" His eyes glinted, as he waited for an anticipated response.

"Mafia! Good heavens!" Colbie paused. "After I'm done eating, do you mind if I take a little tour? I'm writing a book on Italy—a pictorial—and, I'd love to include it!"

The waiter's eyes narrowed. "What's a . . ."

"Pictorial? You know—photos!"

He smiled. "Yes, please!" With that, he left, turning his attention to another table.

After a few bites, Colbie sat back. "I'm already stuffed!"

"Me, too—I wonder if we can take it back to the hotel?"

Colbie glanced at two patrons walking in the door. "Don't look now—but, I think part of the mafia just walked in—is there any way you can get a discreet photo?"

Kevin shook his head. "Not in this light—I'd have to use a flash."

The two men crossed the main dining room floor, disappearing through a narrow door close to the restrooms. "I wonder what's back there," Colbie wondered, unaware she was talking to herself.

There was something about them she couldn't quite place, but one seemed familiar. "I can't imagine I would have seen either one of those guys before," she commented, "but, I could swear the short one was Giuseppe Marino . . ."

Kevin lowered his voice. "I thought the same thing—but, it's not. That guy could be his twin, though . . ."

"It makes me think this is the type of place Marino might come, especially if he's a wannabe tough guy."

"How do you know that?"

She leaned back in her chair. "Because I feel it—that back room? I'm willing to bet regular patrons aren't ever allowed . . ."

Kevin was quiet, unsure if he should play devil's advocate. "Maybe—you don't know that for sure, though. Maybe there are offices back there—or, maybe those two guys own it."

"You sound just like Ryan . . ." She paused. "Maybe . . ." She glanced at the narrow doorway, then focused on Kevin. "But, I doubt it . . ."

CHAPTER

15

*G*eorgia, Kara, and Marguerite checked into one of Milan's little-known hotels ensuring anonymity, as well as privacy—using pseudonyms and paying in cash, no one noticed one was a world-class model.

"They don't recognize me without make up," Marguerite whispered as they entered the elevator. "Especially those outside of the runway . . ."

Giorgia smiled. "It plays to our advantage . . ."

Prior instructions and arrangements dictated silence while in the elevator, or hallways—even though the hotel was under the radar, cameras were strategically placed. Outside of their rooms, they were only tourists on their first trip to the boot-shaped country, expected to act as such.

Inside? A different story.

After checking each for surveillance devices, they agreed to meet in Giorgia's room at nine o'clock that evening, all expected to provide a comprehensive report informing the group of their progress. "He'll arrive at nine-thirty," Giorgia promised, "and, his time is short."

"I didn't prepare anything written," Kara offered. "My report shouldn't take long . . ."

Marguerite nodded. "Smart move—we can't leave any type of paper trail."

"Excellent!" Giorgia paused, realizing their planning was truly about to come to fruition. "Our plan is foolproof—but, only if each of us does our part."

Minutes later, they parted, each consumed with thoughts of what could possibly go wrong.

Everything . . .

"There is dissension . . ." As Gianni Marino spoke, he scanned the room, although there was really no reason for such precautions—privacy was never intruded upon neither physically, nor technologically.

"Tell me . . ."

"Sources tell me Luca Russo is unhappy . . ."

Carmine Bartolo glanced at his watch, fully aware he was to be somewhere else within the hour. "Unhappy about what?"

Gianni said nothing for a moment, recalling his brother's words. "Before we discuss Russo, there's something else." He paused. "Giuseppe knows . . ."

"Knows what?"

"About the girl . . ."

Bartolo's impatience spiked, not appreciating Gianni's dragging out what he could have said in seconds. Again, he glanced at his watch. "I will appreciate getting to the point—I have an appointment, and I cannot be late."

Gianni wasn't necessarily the brightest bulb, but he clearly understood. "In London . . ."

"If you're speaking of Armond Coniglio's sample room girl, I heard . . ."

"Giuseppe was there . . ."

Bartolo's expression flickered recognition, recalling a conversation with his boss a week earlier. "Are you telling me he witnessed the poor girl's murder?"

"Not exactly—he witnessed the arm."

Again, Bartolo cycled the conversation in his mind—the woman who discovered it, and the gentleman who whisked her away before she could say more. "I'm listening. Explain . . ."

Within ten, Gianni brought Carmine Bartolo up to speed about Giuseppe's witnessing Russo's pitching Chiara's arm into the river—leaving out, however, the part about his brother's warning Armond Coniglio about Luca's work being sloppy, and unprofessional. Such honesty wouldn't have played well.

Clearly, it was a piece of news setting Bartolo on edge. "It's unfortunate your brother chose not to bring me into his confidence immediately . . ."

"Agreed—but, in his defense, he's sticking to Russo like glue, as your boss directed. That's why he asked me to tell you—he knew you'd want to know."

Bartolo rose, straightening his jacket. "Tell Giuseppe he did the right thing . . ." With that, he strode through a back door leading to a nondescript alley, his mind juggling thoughts about Luca Russo, and Armond Coniglio. *If,* he thought, *Luca Russo is experiencing difficulties, it may be in our favor . . .*

In approaching darkness, he climbed into a waiting black sedan, barked orders in Italian to the driver, then sat back to think.

Perhaps, it is time to bring him into the fold . . .

"Are you taking leftovers?" Kevin glanced at his still-heaping plate of spaghetti, then at Colbie.

"Are you kidding—I won't eat for a year!"

"Then, I'm guessing you're not up for dessert . . ."

"Nope . . ." Colbie focused on the narrow hall leading to the restrooms. "Did you see those two guys leave?"

"No—they're still in there."

Colbie thought for a moment, her radar ramping up. "I don't think so . . ."

Kevin watched as she worked through what she was feeling—or, seeing. From the time he began working with her, he was always amazed by her accuracy. "Just shut up, and listen," Ryan once told him when he first joined them as an equal partner.

Colbie closed her eyes, allowing intuition to guide her. "There's a back door," she said, feeling strongly neither man was in the building. "Someone picked up one of them—the bigger guy."

"What happened to the other one—the one who looks like Giuseppe Marino?"

"He left on foot . . ." In her vision, she watched as he disappeared down the alley into approaching darkness.

Kevin remained silent until she opened her eyes. "Do you know who they are?"

She shook her head. "No—did you notice anything in particular about them?"

"Other than the shorter guy looking like Giuseppe Marino?" He paused, thinking. "Not really . . ."

Again, Colbie closed her eyes for a moment, the energy of both men still with her. "He's very close to our investigation . . ."

"Do you know how?"

"Not yet—but, he's tied to us somehow."

"Well, now that you mention it, I did notice he was impeccably dressed . . ."

Colbie opened her eyes, focusing on Kevin. "Yes! That's it! He was wearing designer clothes—or, at the very least, they weren't straight off the rack."

"I know I haven't seen him before—but, the fact he's with someone who looks a lot like one of our players?"

"I know—let's get the hell out of here. We have work to do . . ."

Kevin nodded, then stood. "If Giuseppe Marino has a brother, I'm sure as hell going to find out . . ."

"If he does, and the guy I saw walk through the back door is him . . ." Her voice trailed, gut instinct telling her they were on the right track.

"If that's the case, pieces are beginning to fit . . ."

Both headed for the front door, bidding goodbye and thanks to their server. "We need to have a confab—new players are surfacing, and we need to reassess."

Kevin turned to her as they stepped outside. "You know what's weird?"

Colbie looked at him, waiting.

"Our focus is changing from Basile Duchon to . . ."

"Armond Coniglio?"

"Well, yes—but, we always knew Coniglio was the target of our investigation. It kind of seems like our work for Duchon is taking a back seat—when we started, it was all about Duchon's feud with Armond. And, the reason he hired us was because he thinks the industry is rigged . . ." Kevin paused. "Now, it seems we're investigating things that don't have anything to do with that . . ."

Colbie was quiet, knowing his observation had credence. "You're right . . ."

"It's nine-thirty . . ."

"He'll be here—be patient!" Giorgia glanced at Kara who appeared a tad pale. "There's nothing to be nervous about, my dear—all of us know this is the only way."

Kara nodded, unconvinced. When she accepted her position with Basile Duchon, she never considered the possibility of being drawn into a web of deceit. The truth was she didn't sign on for it, and she wasn't sure she wanted to be involved—even so, she knew there was no other choice.

Just as Marguerite checked her watch, a solid rap sounded on the door and, moments later, Giorgia stepped aside as their guest crossed the threshold. "Please—make yourself comfortable." She smiled, then gestured to the most comfortable chair in the room. "As you know, we have much to discuss . . ."

For the next hour, Giorgia, Kara, and Marguerite filled him in on their progress, each commenting there was a need for expediency. "As you know," Marguerite commented, "everything must be in place by the time we reach Paris . . ."

Oscar Hallberg nodded. "It will be—everything is on track." He hesitated, considering whether he should bring up recently received information about Armond Coniglio's right-hand man.

Finally, a decision. "This evening I learned interesting information about Luca Russo—it seems he's dissatisfied with his current arrangement."

Every eyebrow arched. "Dissatisfied with Armond?" Somehow, Giorgia found his statement difficult to believe— he'd been with Coniglio for years, and it was no secret the designer relied on him heavily. Was he Armond's henchman? Perhaps. If so, he was the best dressed strong-arm on the block.

Hallberg nodded. "One must wonder what he will do should he grow weary of Armond's antics . . ."

"I can't imagine that's being the case . . ." Of everyone in the room, Giorgia knew Luca Russo best, and she couldn't think of any situation that would drive a wedge between them.

"Nor could I—until now. Surely you noticed—Armond is not the same man he was only a few years ago. His unceasing desire to take down those who pose a threat to his design empire seems to have become his most recent, targeted passion—and, he will stop at nothing to attain satisfaction. Perhaps he feels Russo is no longer indispensable . . ."

The room was silent as they considered the possibility. "If that's the case," Marguerite finally commented, "Russo can be an important ally for us . . ."

Giorgio was stunned. "Jump ship from Armond Coniglio? Never! Luca Russo isn't stupid—doing such a thing would be a death sentence!"

Again, silence.

CHAPTER

16

Colbie stared at the envelope as she closed her hotel room door. "I don't recognize the handwriting," she commented as she joined Ryan on the couch.

Kevin glanced at both of them. "Is it the same writing as the other two you received?"

"No—not even close." Of course, anyone's natural inclination would be to put speculation to rest as quickly as possible—Colbie, however, wanted to drink in everything about the writing. Paper. Pen preference.

The script was significantly different than the note she received in New York, and London. "Whoever wrote this," she determined, holding the envelope up to the light, "probably prefers roller point to ball point . . ."

Again, Kevin glanced at Ryan. "How do you know?"

"Look . . ." She pointed to her name. "It's a much thinner stroke than a ballpoint . . ."

"Maybe—but, what's to say whoever wrote it didn't use the only pen available?"

Ryan nodded. "You mean like a regular pen in a hotel room . . ."

"Exactly!"

Colbie thought for a moment. "Good point—so, shall we see what it has to say?"

Without waiting for their answer, she carefully slit the top of the envelope with the hotel letter opener, a faint fragrance of men's cologne triggering her senses. Extracting what appeared to be high-end paper, the assaulting scrawl in a seemingly man's handwriting instantly alerted her to something possibly integral in their investigation.

Valentine,

Perhaps you have time in your busy schedule to meet— tomorrow afternoon before the evening runway?

Luca Russo

Silence.

Finally, Ryan took the note from her. "Did he say where?"

Colbie shook her head. "No—but, as you can see, he left what I can only assume is his personal cell."

Again, silence.

Kevin considered keeping his mouth shut, but it wasn't in his nature. "Are you going to go?"

Colbie turned her attention to him. "Of course! You don't think I'm going to pass up such an opportunity, do you? There's no reason I shouldn't go . . ."

Ryan shot Kevin a sideways glance. "You have a lot to learn, son . . ."

Kevin stood, grinning. "Apparently . . ."

Moments later he and Ryan were out the door, leaving Colbie to consider the reason for Luca Russo's wanting to meet. *It has to be something important*, she thought as she slipped off her shoes, then headed for a hot shower.

Really important . . .

The note made for a restless sleep and, by seven the following morning, Colbie was up, dressed, and on her first cup of coffee. Several times throughout the night, she tried tapping into her intuitive senses, but without a flicker of information.

Gently pulling the note from the envelope, it's paper a fine, elegant linen, she closed her eyes, attempting to tap into Russo. *He already knows where I'm staying,* she thought, her fingers lingering on the paper's texture, *so the hotel's phone won't provide additional information. My cell? A little too personal* . . . Still, she preferred to have a verbatim record of their conversation—or, text.

Decision made, she quickly tapped a text to the number provided in the note, then waited. Of course, she couldn't be certain the number was a cell, but, if not, it would only be seconds until she'd receive an error message.

Within moments, the screen illuminated with a time, and place. Quickly, she responded her confirmation—after that?

Nothing.

Madelinne smoothed her skirt as she sat. "What is it you need, Armond? I have an appointment within the hour, and I have little time . . ."

Coniglio fussed with a vase of fresh, creamy white calla lilies until they were just so, amused by such amateur false bravado—then, his eyes met hers. Although their personal relationship was behind them, he still knew her better than anyone—and, there was clearly something she was keeping from him.

"It's come to my attention you're seeing someone . . ."

"Someone? Surely you can be more definitive . . ." She met his gaze, refusing to allow satisfaction. "Besides, what if I am? You're no longer in my life, Armond—other than business, perhaps—I fail to understand what my personal life has to do with you."

Coniglio smiled, his disdain obvious in uncomfortable, momentary silence. "Oh, but it does—surely, you must realize those in my life never stray."

"Stray? You make it sound like I'm a dog on the street knowing where to get my next meal . . . "

A smile. "Perhaps an apt interpretation . . ." He paused, tracing the elegant neck of one flower with his index finger. "Who is he?"

"Armond—what I do, say, or otherwise is none of your concern. If I choose to see someone, I will—and, I don't require your permission to do so."

"I don't care for your tone . . ."

Madelinne stood. "How unfortunate for you—luckily, what you think is none of my business."

Coniglio said nothing as he watched who he considered a so-so designer headed for the door. "Leaving so soon?" He smiled, knowing he hit a nerve.

"I have a busy day, as I said—and, this conversation doesn't interest me." She turned, eyeing him, fingers resting lightly on the door latch. "I hear you're finding yourself in a rather precarious position . . ."

"Meaning . . ."

She smiled. "I think you know . . ." With that, she stepped across the threshold, closing the door softly.

Armond Coniglio watched, anger bristling as her dismissal of him confirmed his thoughts—his reason for demanding a meeting. There was no question his former paramour was shooting her mouth off, and it was to someone he didn't know—and, if it weren't for one of the patternmakers in his sample room, he'd be none the wiser.

He tapped the screen on his cell, then waited. Moment's later, connected. "What can I do for you, Armond?" Within five, his call faded to dead air, each understanding there was work to be done.

Luca Russo was one of those guys whose hair was never out of place—he made certain of it. It was odd, too—growing up, he never gave a rat's ass about what he wore, or how he looked. With little money to spare, an impeccable wardrobe wasn't at the top of his list—until he exhibited a bent toward fashion design when he flipped into his early twenties.

Always strikingly handsome, natural instinct to make the most of his assets kicked into high gear when he had an opportunity to keep company with a tall, willowy model who was barely out of her second decade. It didn't take long to realize hers was a life in which he would do well and, from then on, he did everything he could to ingratiate himself to those who were decision makers within the industry. But, it wasn't until he attended his first private cocktail party, chatting it up with the big guns, did he fully realize his calling. It wasn't to be a model, designer, or anything else requiring a specific set of skills. No—what he brought to the party was more in the private security arena.

Working his way through the ranks, it was a solid two years before Armond Coniglio gave him a second look. As much as Russo tried, throughout his freshman years in the biz, Coniglio dismissed him as he would a pesky fly. But, giving up? Never. Luca Russo knew unequivocally he could run the designer's operation with a silken iron fist, never hesitating to perform any job needing done.

Even so, Armond didn't get the hint, and it was only after losing one of his top men did Coniglio decide to give Russo a shot. A private conversation later and a wad of cash to go with it, Russo finally realized his dream, joining the ranks of those who preceded him. He, however, had the looks and an eye for class, standing him apart from others in his particular line of work. Deciding early on he'd never play the part of a thug, his sleek manner of doing business earned him an honored seat at Armond Coniglio's table by the end of his first year in the designer's employ. By the tenth year? A place at Armond's side. Until, that is, Coniglio and Luca began to sense a burgeoning chasm in their professional relationship.

An undeniable fracture.

At first, it was barely noticeable—just an occasional feeling of unease when asked to perform certain tasks. As years passed, however, Russo wasn't the only one noticing Armond Coniglio's personality shift, and those exhibiting an alarming lack of common sense and poor taste to mention it were met with instant dismissal—from his employ, and personal life. But, it was only when Armond ordered him to relieve the tension in his life created by Chiara Ricci did Russo begin to consider Armond's mental acuity. Of course, he'd carried out unsavory tasks previously, but nothing to the extent of the young woman from the sample room—it was something he considered despicable, and unpleasant. Framing Basile Duchon was one thing—murder was another.

Yet, he complied.

Doing so brought out—front and center—a part of his personality he didn't particularly like. Always careful to keep it under wraps, thoughts of changing circumstances began to play in his mind, and those who knew him from a lifetime ago noticed their friend was only a shadow of someone they recognized.

There was talk.

"What's going on with Luca," several asked over cocktails, their voices lowered to furtive whispers. Of course, most declined to comment, but there were those indiscriminate few who did—and, it was because of them Oscar Hallberg caught wind of Russo's dissatisfaction with his current situation—it was then things changed.

It was then new plans were put in motion.

Colbie made it a point to make an appearance at the last day of the Milan show, playing her part to perfection—unable, however, to divert her thoughts from Luca Russo to the task at hand. The fact he contacted her was intriguing enough—but, she couldn't help feeling there was an undercurrent of something she didn't understand.

Ryan, of course, strongly suggested Kevin accompany her—something Colbie immediately dismissed. "If I don't show up alone, all bets are off . . ."

"Well, if you'd been listening, you'd know I didn't say Kevin should go with you—I meant he should keep you in his sight."

There was a tone in Ryan's voice she didn't like. "You mean like Cape Town?"

"That's exactly what I mean . . ."

There it was, again—an edge in his voice, crystallizing her suspicion something was on his mind, yet she knew he was right. He was always concerned for her safety, and the thought of tangling with Italian authorities was an experience she didn't need. "Okay—but, Kevin shouldn't be the one to go with me." She paused. "Russo knows what he looks like—if he catches wind he's under surveillance?"

Ryan nodded. "Agreed—although, I think Kevin should be in a location where he can shoot a few pics. Just in case we need them down the road . . ."

"Are you going to wear a wire," Kevin asked.

Colbie glanced at Ryan. "Well . . ."

"I think you should," Kevin continued. "It's a public place, so there's no danger of your being in a situation where it's discovered . . ."

Again, Ryan agreed. "This is one of those few times you get to record everything without fear of discovery . . ."

Colbie was quiet, thinking. Finally, she checked her watch. "Let's do it—but, we don't have much time. Kevin, get your stuff, so I can get geared up." Then, she focused on Ryan. "Do you know what's across the street from the bistro?"

"No—but, I'm sure I'll find something suitable. All you have to worry about is steering the conversation in the direction it needs to go . . ."

"I know—but, don't forget he's the one who contacted me. There's something he needs to discuss, and I'm going to play it by ear—don't forget, he doesn't have any idea of my real identity, and he's expecting me to be a fashion writer. Nothing else . . ."

Surveillance techniques decided, once Colbie was on board, each left the hotel separately, Kevin heading back to his hotel, then returning with needed equipment as Ryan located the best stakeout location. Wired for sound, Colbie left thirty minutes later, heading directly to the small bistro Luca recommended in his text.

As she pulled open the door, she scanned the area, noticing neither Ryan, nor Kevin. *Perfect . . .*

Then, the voice as smooth as his style. "Ms. Valentine! You look stunning . . ." Luca greeted her with an obligatory cheek-to-cheek.

"Thank you—I appreciate the compliment. I was, however, surprised when I received your message. I had the distinct impression you weren't pleased with me when I interviewed Armond . . ."

Gesturing toward a small table for two toward the back of the restaurant, Russo pulled out her chair as the hostess asked if they wanted to begin their meal with a cocktail. Without asking Colbie her preference, Luca ordered two glasses of a local, Italian wine. "I hope you don't mind," he commented as he pulled out her chair.

"Not in the least . . ."

He took his place in the seat next to her—something Colbie found odd, and pointedly disquieting. She didn't enjoy his being so close to her personal space, but, considering the circumstances, there was nothing she could do. "Now," she began, placing the menu to the side of her plate, "why don't you tell me why you need to see me . . ."

Kevin listened from his position only yards from the bistro's front door, eyebrows arching at Colbie's audacity. *Nothing like getting down to it*, he thought as he adjusted the mix and volume to account for background noise.

Luca smiled. "Right to the point—I like that." He paused, considering his approach. "I shall return the favor—before I do, however, I'd like to thank you for meeting me on such short notice."

Colbie watched as their server placed two wine goblets on the table, then poured a taste before she continued. "Not a problem . . ."

"Again—much appreciated." He paused, took a small sip, nodding approval to the server. Then, he continued. "As you know, I've worked for Armond Coniglio for many years —decades.

"Yes—I can only imagine how difficult your job must be."

"Difficult? Perhaps—but, there are many things to take into consideration when in one's employ."

Colbie sipped her wine, then buttered a piece of Italian bread. "Such as?"

"Suffice it to say there are things that don't come naturally . . ."

"Thing's making you uncomfortable?"

Luca was quiet, suddenly feeling as if he were about to spill his guts about his life's indiscretions. "I trust our conversation is off the record . . ."

Colbie nodded. "Of course . . ."

"Before we begin our discussion, however, there is something I must know . . ."

"And, that is?"

"Your true identity . . ."

She stopped buttering. "I'm not sure what you mean . . ."

"Please—it was clear from the first time we met you're not a journalist. In fact, there's nothing about you suggesting you're familiar with the fashion industry . . ."

Kevin listened, unaware he was holding his breath, then a quick text to Ryan, advising of the conversation. The response was brief. *Keep your ears on . . .*

Colbie placed her glass on the table, refusing to give up her ruse. "Mr. Russo . . ."

"If we're to have an intimate conversation, I insist you call me Luca . . ."

"Alright—Luca. I assure you my writing credentials are solid . . ." She paused. "Is that what this meeting is about? My freelance writing?"

He smiled. "Of course not—I was hoping, though, you would trust me enough to be yourself."

Again, Colbie refused to confirm. "What is it you need to tell me, Luca?"

Russo leveled a serious look. "There is much . . ."

For the next two hours they talked, Luca—for the first time in years—opening up about his position with Armond Coniglio, as well as regrets to go with it. By the time they parted at the bistro's front door, there was a resolution she hadn't seen before.

"I told you where to look—now, it is your job to make things happen."

Colbie said nothing, waiting for him to continue.

"There are three main players—it is up to you to figure out their identity. It shouldn't be difficult—especially considering your special talent."

"What special talent is that?"

"I think you know—Ms. Colleen."

CHAPTER

17

*S*imilar to Chiara, Madelinne Gastineau's body was fished from the drink, Italian police combing the riverbank shortly thereafter for obvious clues. Well—it was similar except for the fact Madelinne was still in one piece.

Their's wasn't an easy task—a cold drizzle kept temps barely above freezing, making the search difficult. By the time the grisly scene hit local news, conditions worsened, forcing the chief investigator to take refuge in a makeshift tent as he considered first facts. "Who is she," he asked, watching his greenhorn inspector blanch to a color resembling fireplace ash. "Get used to it, Marco. It never gets any easier . . ."

A cough. "Madelinne Gastineau, Sir."

"Do we know anything?"

"Not yet, Sir."

And, that was that.

With little to go on, the chief inspector gathered his men, barked a few orders, then took off for parts unknown.

The last thing he needed was quality time with the press.

By the time Colbie reached her hotel, darkness settled on the city, unsavory weather casting a sense of unsettling unease, matching her take on the conversation with Luca Russo. There was no question when he dropped the bomb about her identity, it was a targeted, direct hit. *But, if that's the case,* she wondered as she inserted the key card in her door, *what was the point of meeting with me?*

A quick shower and cup of hot chocolate later, she plopped on the couch, shooting off texts to Ryan and Kevin. From the time she left Russo, there was little opportunity to discuss the conversation, so they were on to Plan B—meet back at the hotel at six-thirty to debrief.

Within ten, they made themselves comfortable, notepads ready. Colbie glanced at Ryan, then Kevin. "Okay—how the hell did Luca Russo know who I am?"

"I have no idea," Ryan commented. "But, what I want to know is how long has he known your name?"

Kevin remained silent, listening as they debated answers they couldn't possibly know. From his perspective? Someone had an intellectual bead on Colbie, targeting her long before they reached Milan. "Do you think it's the same person who sent you the Valentine notes?"

Colbie glanced at Ryan. "I hadn't thought of that . . ."

"It makes sense," Kevin continued. "There's clearly one person who knows who you are—and, that makes me wonder how many other people know the same thing."

"If there is more than one person," Ryan weighed in, "that means one thing . . ."

"Conspiracy . . ." Colbie looked at each of them. "If that's the case, we're nothing, but pawns . . ."

"What do you mean?"

"Well—think about it. Let's say more than one person knows who I am. That means they probably know who you are, too—but, how could they have found out?"

"I think," Kevin interjected, "the only way they could possibly know who you are is through Basile Duchon . . ."

A punch in the gut.

Colbie said nothing, thinking of the possibility Duchon played her for an idiot. "If that's the case, why didn't I pick up on his duplicity?" A pause. "I should have sensed it . . ."

"Not necessarily . . ." Ryan tapped his laptop to life. "Let's figure out who's been in Duchon's life before we came into the picture."

Kevin's eyebrows flipped north. "How the hell are we going to know that? We combed the Internet before we started this gig, and there was nothing about Duchon's being chummy-chummy with anyone!"

"True—so, what's your idea?"

Colbie listened as her partners hashed out possible scenarios before taking charge. "Let's go over everyone we've come in contact with since we started this case—people within the industry." She paused, thinking. "The first person we met in New York was Madelinne, I think . . ."

"Don't forget you got your first Valentine note when we checked into the hotel . . ."

"You're right . . . " Colbie was quiet for a few moments. "When we narrow it down, it's clear someone knew we were in the mix."

Ryan shook his head. "Maybe—if that's the case, why didn't the note read 'Colbie?'"

Silence.

"The more I think about this, the more it stinks," Colbie finally commented. She rose, grabbed a bottle of water from the fridge, then returned to the couch. "And, I for one, don't like being played for a fool . . ."

"Did you hear?"

Colbie barely opened one eye as she looked at the clock on her cell. "Hear what?" Instantly, she sensed something was wrong.

"Madelinne—she's dead."

"What?"

"They found her body last night . . . "

Colbie was quiet, knowing Ryan had a special connection with her. "Are you okay?"

Ryan smiled, although she couldn't see. "I guess . . ." A pause. "I'm fine—hearing it on the news this morning was a hell of a shock, though . . ."

"What happened?"

"Well, as you might imagine, they don't know much, other than her identity."

"Signs of foul play?"

"I don't know—turn on the tube. It's everywhere . . ."

"Let's meet at nine," Colbie suggested.

"I'll tell Kevin . . ."

With that, they clicked off, both thinking of how their case changed within twenty-four hours. *I don't like it,* Colbie thought as she climbed out of bed. *I don't like it one damned bit . . .*

Chief Inspector Santoro looked remarkably refreshed as he started his day, the only thing of importance being a young designer's body stuck on a bridge pylon for all to see the prior evening. It wasn't until he walked through his office door that morning did he learn of her vocation, and he was waiting on the coroner's report.

Until then, he had nothing.

"Sir?" Inspector Marco poked his head in boss's office door, his face telegraphing he was sorry for the interruption.

"Ah—Marco! What do you have for me?"

"It's in . . ."

"The report?"

Marco nodded, then stepped into the office, handing the file to his superior.

"Did you look at it?"

"Not yet, Sir—I figured you should be the first to lay eyes on it."

Santoro nodded, then flipped open the folder, scanning its contents. "Gunshot to the back of the head . . ." He was quiet for a moment, wondering what could have upset someone so much to resort to murder. Execution.

The double tap.

"Get me all you can on her—I find it strange one from the fashion industry is found wrapped around a pylon just when the town is buzzing because of the show . . ."

Inspector Marco nodded. "Yes, Sir—anything else?"

The chief inspector eyed him, considering whether the young man standing before him had the chops to make it in their line of business. "No. Bring me something by the end of the day . . ."

Luca Russo couldn't get Colbie Colleen out of his mind. Of course, what he told her during their afternoon meeting was a complete line of bullshit, his intent to bait her by confiding confidentialities regarding his life. What he really wanted?

Confirmation.

Received.

He, however, was in the same boat as Colbie, Ryan, and Kevin, all wanting to know why she was hired. The only leg up Colbie had on him was knowing Basile Duchon brought her into the mix.

He stepped in front of the foyer mirror, adjusting his tie, then fiddled with the vase of slender flowers set strategically to the side, its reflection resembling a piece of art.

Then, his thoughts turned to Madelinne Gastineau.

The whole thing was so bloody unpleasant—he never considered for a moment she would fight back. In the end, however, he prevailed, thinking the flower was a nice touch. It added a element of—respect—for an otherwise distasteful situation. *It's a pity*, he thought as he leaned forward to inspect a long scratch on his cheek. *She really was quite talented . . .*

Giorgia stared at the television screen, uncertain she heard correctly. Clearly, the report had to be true, triggering a warning—one she must heed. *It's only a matter of time*, she thought, until they looked into Chiara Ricci's murder—*how*

can they not? In one way, however, their doing so could be a good thing—in another, it would bring the underbelly of the fashion industry into the limelight once again.

That meant taking names.

As she listened to the reporter describe the scene, her cell vibrated. "Marguerite—did you hear?"

"Indeed—that's why I'm calling. We must take great care . . ."

"I agree. Meet me this afternoon—let Kara know. I'll contact Oscar . . ."

Moments later plans were in motion.

Changes.

CHAPTER

18

Marco peeked his head around the door. "Sir?"

"What do you have, Marco . . ."

"More information about the victim, Sir . . ." He watched his boss, waiting for an indication he was to put the folder on his desk, then get the hell out of there.

"Sit . . ."

The young inspector obeyed, taking a seat on the only other chair in the room.

"What do I need to know?"

"Well, Sir—Madelinne Gastineau was pretty well known in the fashion world, although she hadn't risen to the height of a household name."

"What else?"

"She was in her mid-thirties—and, for a while, she was a model until she decided to design clothes. Not so long ago, she was an item with Armond Coniglio . . ."

"How do you know that?"

"The Internet—it appears they had a falling out of some sort about a year ago, and that's when she decided to launch her own fashion collection. That's why she was here—her designs were getting rave reviews in New York and London, and she was traveling the circuit."

"Why did she and Coniglio split the sheets?"

"Who knows? Both were tight lipped about it when it hit the wires, so it kind of faded into a nothing story . . ."

Chief Inspector Santoro sat back in his chair, then tossed his pen on the desk. "Is that all?"

Marco shook his head. "One more thing . . ."

"Tell me . . ."

"It seems one of Coniglio's patternmakers was murdered during the run of the London Fashion Week show . . ."

That's when Santoro's wheels started turning.

Two murders in the span of a couple of weeks? Murders within the same industry? Even a complete moron would see the connection . . .

Finally! Something to chew on!

By the end of the week, collections were in the process of being packed for shipment, designers looking forward to the final show in the top four. Coniglio, Hallberg, and Duchon were emerging as the top designer names for the winter season, while several designers expecting more than platitudes tried to figure out what went wrong.

As Colbie, Ryan, and Kevin prepared to travel to Paris, neither felt the surge of excitement of the previous shows. "I don't know," Kevin commented as they packed their business belongings, "this whole fashion business seems like nothing but a big, fat search for identity . . ."

Colbie stopped, looking at him. "Meaning?"

"I mean everyone wants to be recognized—you know, make it to the top. As far as I can see, it's ain't so great up there . . ."

"I suppose, though, you could say the same thing about any business."

"Maybe—but, this feels completely different." He paused, considering whether he should broach a question. "Who do you think offed Chiara and Madelinne," he finally asked. "I know you well enough by now to know you have an idea . . ."

Colbie tossed him a folder crammed with case notes. "Make sure you know where that is," she laughed. "I have a feeling we're going to need it!"

Kevin grinned. "Don't I always?" Again, he paused. "I'm serious, though—who do you think killed Chiara, and Madelinne?"

Colbie plopped on the couch, kicking off her shoes. "I don't know—I have a few ideas, but I don't know anything for certain."

"I find it interesting the two killed were people familiar to us . . ."

"True—but, when you think about it, Ryan was the only one they knew."

"Well, kind of—don't forget we met Madelinne in New York."

Colbie nodded. "That's right—but, Ryan was getting to know her."

Both were quiet for a moment. Finally, Kevin sat across from her in an easy chair. "Okay—how about if I go first?" He didn't wait for an answer, even though he knew he may be getting a bit pushy for Colbie's taste. "I can count my suspects on one hand," he announced, holding up his thumb. "First on my list is someone associated with Armond Coniglio . . ."

"Okay—let's work through it. We know Armond had dalliances with more than one designer throughout the years. Some publicized more than others . . ."

"That's right—I don't know anything about Chiara, but we know for a fact Madelinne Gastineau was seen about town with Coniglio more than once."

Colbie was quiet. "But, what about Chiara? Coniglio wouldn't lower himself to fraternizing with someone from his sample room . . ."

"I think Coniglio regarded her as collateral damage."

"Collateral damage for what?"

"Well—what if Chiara knew something about Armond?"

"You mean something he wanted to keep private?"

"Exactly . . ."

Colbie gazed out the hotel window, considering Kevin's hypothesis. "So, you're saying she was murdered to shut her up about something . . ."

"Maybe—at least, it makes some sense."

"What would that be, though? I find it difficult to believe Chiara would have such information. How would she get it?"

"Madelinne. You know they were close—what if Madelinne confided in Chiara about her relationship with Coniglio?"

"If that's the case, I doubt Madelinne would have opened her mouth about it. That seems risky . . ."

Kevin nodded. "True—okay, that's number one. Second on my list? Luca Russo . . ."

"Why him?"

"Why not?"

Colbie had to agree. There was something not settling right as she recalled their conversation at the bistro. It was clear Russo's real purpose for inviting her was to reveal her true identity.

Everything else was probably a bunch of crap.

"I can't argue your point—I agree something isn't right with Russo, and the whole time we were talking? I felt as if he were handing me a line of total bullshit . . ."

With the whirlwind of Milan Fashion Week closing, it was the first time she had time to discuss her conversation with Russo. What Ryan thought, she had no idea—but, there was no question Kevin's possible scenarios about who murdered Chiara and Madelinne held water.

Kevin eyed her. "So—how are we going to approach it in Paris? It's kind of like our case is going full circle . . ."

Colbie nodded. "Agreed. I have no doubt Duchon is at the center of things . . ."

He stood, then grabbed another file. "Don't you think it's about time we find out?"

CHAPTER

19

asile Duchon stood at his hotel suite's window, gazing down at the reflection of streetlights on a wet, dank street. "It's colder than usual this time of year," he commented, turning to the young woman sitting in a chair next to the marble fireplace.

"As much as I would like to discuss the inclement weather, Basile, it is not the reason I requested our meeting this evening . . ."

"Then, why are you here?"

"Because we are running out of time." She paused, gauging his response. "I'm curious—how do you assess

Colbie Colleen's performance?" The lanky model paused, her cocoa-colored eyes flashing with subtle irritation. "It seems she's completely ineffectual . . ."

"We speak regularly—but, I agree. Our intent is not being met . . ." Duchon sighed, clearly aware his decision to hire the investigator from the States was an egregious error.

"What do you intend?"

"As of now? Nothing. I'm not yet ready to give up— we know Armond Coniglio is at the center of my career's demise, as does Mademoiselle Colleen. I maintain hope she can complete her task to our satisfaction . . ."

Marguerite was silent, knowing there was little time to effect their plan. "Kara is our ace in the hole—I suggest she has a meeting with your investigator, making sure she's pointed in the right direction. As of now, the lovely Colbie Colleen is running in circles . . ."

Again, Basile sighed as he signaled it was time for her to leave. Ushering her to the door, he knew they were running out of time. "Arangez-vous pour que cela arrive . . ."

"We have one week," Colbie reiterated as she unlocked her business only travel case. "So, get ready for no sleep—I have a feeling it's going to be an around-the-clock seven days . . ."

"Then, let's get to work . . ." Ryan suggested, popping the final bite of a croissant in his mouth. "I'm ready!"

"Me, too—I have a feeling this is going to be a good week!" Kevin glanced at both of them, his laptop ready.

Colbie smiled, thinking about her newest partner. There was something about him she found engaging, and signs of his intuitive abilities were beginning to surface. Time together during the month of winter fashion weeks revealed a gentle young man who probably didn't have any idea he was a sensitive—and, Colbie wasn't sure if it were up to her to tell him.

So, for the remainder of the only day available to plan their week, the three of them hashed out what they knew—as well as what they thought they knew—about Armond Coniglio's involvement regarding Basile Duchon's cataclysmic demise within the fashion industry. "We have the players," Colbie commented, "but, I feel as if we're missing something."

"Or, someone . . ." Ryan glanced at Kevin. "It seems to me Coniglio is dispensing of those who may be opposing him in some way." He paused. "Of course, I don't know that for sure, but the murder of two people within his employ?"

Kevin nodded. "Or, former employ. I agree—but, the question is why is he bumping them off?"

"Or, having someone else do it. You know Armond Coniglio doesn't strike me as the type who would dirty his hands with such unpleasantness . . ."

"Russo?"

"He's my best guess—both of you heard the conversation we had at the bistro before we left Milan. I'm sure the whole sob story was bogus . . ."

"That may be," Ryan interjected, "but, the real question is does he think you believed it? If he does, that places us in a good position . . ."

"Well, there's no doubt he's growing increasingly weary of Armond Coniglio, and I got a strong feeling something's about to happen where that relationship's concerned."

Kevin shook his head. "I don't know—I still think there's someone in the mix we haven't considered." He glanced at both of them. "But, I also feel it's someone with a whole lot to lose . . ."

Colbie was quiet for a moment, thinking. "Any idea of who that is?"

"Maybe. I think we need to focus on three things . . ."

Ryan glanced at Colbie. "And, those are?"

"The top three designers—Coniglio, Duchon, and Hallberg."

"Hallberg?" Ryan caught Colbie's surprise in his peripheral vision. "What on earth does Oscar Hallberg have to do with any of this?"

Kevin looked to Colbie for confirmation. "What do you think?"

Again, Colbie took her time to answer. "I think . . . you have a point. Oscar Hallberg has been under our radar since we began the investigation." She focused on Kevin. "Until you brought it up, I hadn't really considered him—but, perhaps it's time we do."

An hour later, as they were preparing to break for the evening, a sharp rap on the hotel room door interrupted their brief, concentrated silence. "Are you expecting someone," Colbie asked as she headed for the door.

"Not me," Ryan and Kevin answered in unison.

Moments later she returned, envelope in hand.

"Not again!" Ryan glanced at Kevin. "Did we ever figure out for certain who was sending the Valentine notes?"

Kevin shook his head as Colbie sat, opening the envelope with her index finger. "It's from Kara Vaughn! She wants to schedule a meeting . . ."

"Why?" Ryan didn't take his eyes off of Colbie as she reread the note. As a result of his years working with her, he knew when her intuition was propelled into high gear, as well as every little tell.

"She doesn't say—but, there's an address and time, so I'm guessing it's about something important."

The three sat in silence for several moments, wondering what a bit player for Basile Duchon's organization could possibly have to do with their case—a point Ryan was quick to point out. "I don't know—don't forget Duchon played you. He could be setting you up . . ."

Kevin's concerned look made her think twice. "Maybe—but, I don't think so."

"Why?"

"Because we're nearing the end of our investigation—remember, we only have one week left, and we don't have much to show. At least, nothing concrete, and the fact is we're spinning our wheels . . ."

Kevin's frown signaled he wasn't quite buying it. "That may be true, but what does Kara Vaughn have to do with anything? If I recall correctly, she's the one who sources all of Basile's fabrics . . ."

"Yes—but, don't forget she also worked for Armond Coniglio in a similar position. She's the creme de la creme when it comes to fabrics—someone with her knowledge is probably worth a pretty penny. She's hardly a bit player . . ."

"I still don't get it . . ." Clearly, Kevin wasn't ready to drop it. "What does fabric have to do with Duchon's fall from grace? Or, for that matter, two murders!"

Ryan listened as they duked it out, enjoying Kevin's fresh approach to Colbie's assessment, figuring there weren't many people who had the guts to challenge her. Both had reasonable arguments, but, when it came down to it, he'd put his money on Colbie every time.

Finally, she was ready to call it a night. "We're not going to have the answer to that question until tomorrow—so, in the meantime, I have to get my beauty sleep." She rose, heading for the main bedroom in the suite. "You can show yourselves out . . ."

As was always his practice, Armond Coniglio stood in front of the full length mirror in his suite's bedroom, admiring his reflection. Gently, he arranged his signature flower on his lapel, keenly aware it signified everything for which he worked diligently. Only a few knew of his pursuit to present a stunning collection—one taking the breath from those who had the privilege to view it in person.

Carefully chosen for their ability to create as well as keep their mouths shut, those within his inner circle amplified his mounting excitement as the final, winter Fashion Week commenced. *It will be like no other*, he thought, straightening his silk tie. *I will maintain my rightful place as the world's most revered designer* . . .

The only thing standing in his way of unbridled success, however, was the man he once considered blood. Someone who would step up whenever needed.

Someone he could trust.

Unfortunately, theirs was a relationship in danger of fracturing completely.

As he admired what he created as well as himself, his decision took root—one bringing no joy, but filled with necessity. Pleasure or happiness, he knew, weren't his tantamount goals.

Only power could provide what he craved.

Kara requested an early meeting and, as Colbie waited in a local hotel's restaurant, she recalled their initial conversation. A lovely, middle-aged woman, there was nothing about her signaling she was wrapped up in something most likely out of her league, and she certainly didn't give off the vibe of needing to be on Colbie's radar.

"Ms. Valentine?"

Colbie turned to greet the woman who reminded her of an aunt she cherished—soft features and English skin made her look younger than she probably was, and Colbie couldn't help thinking she should be so lucky. "Kara! How wonderful to see you!"

"Thank you for agreeing to meet me. I know it was short notice . . ."

"Well, it's better than no notice!" Colbie gestured to the seat across from her. "Please—sit. I'm guessing we have something to discuss . . ."

Moments later, they faced each other, neither quite certain where to begin. Finally, Kara took the lead. "I'm sure you're wondering why I contacted you . . ."

"Well—yes. We only met briefly in New York, so I can't imagine why you need to see me . . ."

Kara was quiet, then signaled the server, both women ordering tea, and a croissant. "Before we go further, I think we should be honest with each other . . . Ms. Colleen."

Colbie eyed her, again wondering how many knew her true identity. "How did you find out?"

"Basile—at the beginning of your investigation, he was quite thrilled with the idea of your being on board."

"And, now?"

Kara watched as the server placed their breakfasts in front of them, then left so they could discuss whatever it was seeming so serious. "Now—he still believes you can discover Armond Coniglio's part in destroying his career." She paused. "As you can imagine, no one enjoys being accused of fraud—Basile included."

Colbie sipped her tea, then asked the question to which she desperately needed the answer. "I suspected my task has nothing to do with the fashion industry's being rigged . . ."

"Basile's idea . . ."

"Who else knows of my true identity?"

Kara smiled. "Only a few—Basile, of course, as well as Giorgia Mancini, and Marguerite Villanova."

Colbie said nothing, letting the information settle. She was stunned by the admission two people she never considered being involved were in it up to their eyeballs. "Don't forget Luca Russo," she prompted, knowing the way she phrased her question would elicit a specific response.

"Luca? Are you sure?"

There it was—confirmation Coniglio's camp wasn't intertwined with Duchon's. "Oh, yes—I'm sure." Colbie paused. "Now, Kara—why don't you tell me why I'm here."

"I see your surprise—well, I don't blame you. Basile and Marguerite insisted you know nothing, thereby ensuring the integrity of your investigation."

"Basile, and Marguerite? What about you?"

"I knew nothing until later—in fact, when I first met you, I had no idea you were investigating Armond." She paused. "I wasn't happy about it, either . . ."

"Being involved, or not knowing my identity?"

Kara smiled slightly. "Both, really—but, when I fully realized what Armond is capable of, I knew they were doing the right thing."

Colbie took another sip of tea, then a bite of her croissant. "The right thing about what?"

"I suppose it will help if I start at the beginning—when I was employed by Armond."

"Okay—shoot. I'm listening . . ."

"Well, as you already know, I was employed by Armond in much the same capacity as I am now with Basile's organization . . ."

"If I recall correctly, you're the top gun when it comes to sourcing fabrics . . ."

Kara laughed. "I don't know about that—but, for some reason, I have a gift for spotting the truly unique."

Colbie glanced at Kara's fingers as she sipped her tea— long and elegant. Her skin was like porcelain—what Colbie's grandmother would have called a 'fine hand.' "So—you worked for Armond. Why did you choose to leave?"

"I was beginning to suspect something was off . . ."

"With him? His collection?"

"Sort of—after I returned from a three-month excursion sourcing fabrics for him, it was then I noticed several bolts in his private design suite were unlike anything I'd seen."

Colbie put her cup down, leveling a serious look at the woman across from her. "I don't understand—what does fabric have to do with the reason I'm investigating Armond Coniglio?"

Kara didn't take her eyes from Colbie's. "As I said, when you were hired, it had nothing to do with infiltrating Armond's organization because of suspicions of his rigging the shows . . ."

"Then, what?

"Fraud . . . pure, and simple."

CHAPTER

20

*O*scar Hallberg glanced at the text on his cell screen, notifying him the meeting was in progress. Quickly, he tapped. *Proceed. Do not deviate from the plan . . .*

As he awaited a response—if there were one—thoughts turned to coming days. If everything proceeded according to plan, there would be a new king of the mountain in the design industry—a deserved king. Ever since his meeting with Duchon weeks prior, it was prudent to give considerable thought to their circumstances—Basile's plan, however, wasn't particularly well thought out. There were holes allowing for dire consequences—the sole reason he didn't immediately comply with Duchon's request to join forces.

That didn't mean, however, he couldn't create his own formidable force—which he did, unbeknownst to Duchon. It was no secret Duchon's health was fragile, and one couldn't help but consider his mental health may not be far behind. Everything about him was compromised, and living as a hermit virtually underground didn't help. So, it was when he met Duchon that day only a few weeks prior did Oscar realize someone needed to take the helm.

Someone competent.

Decision made, it wasn't difficult to figure out who stood as Duchon's compatriots willing to join him in his scheme to make Armond Coniglio pay for disgracing the design industry and Duchon, as well as destroying his career. Once he targeted Giorgia Mancini, everyone else fell in line, Marguerite the most vocal about her disdain for Coniglio. She, too, was noticing Duchon's actions were suspect, and doubt crept into their conversations more often than not. When Hallberg's offer to join him in taking down the Almighty Armond was placed in her lap, there wasn't the slightest hesitation.

'Revenge' proved a powerful word.

Kara Vaughn, on the other hand, was more difficult to convince—still, once she learned of Armond's duplicity, convincing her to join the Hallberg ranks proved easier. Together, they formed a powerful triumvirate, guided by the man who had much to gain.

And, lose.

Luca Russo slit the envelope along the top, curiosity piqued. As he extracted a simple, white note card, he noticed its fine grain, similar to his own preferences.

Luca,

Please meet me tomorrow, 3:00 P.M. at the coffee shop—you know the one.

Oscar

Without thought—or, second read—he tucked it into his suit coat pocket, then smoothed his hair.

There was much to do.

Chief Inspector Santoro sat at his desk, thinking about Madelinne Gastineau—and, Chiara Ricci. One never to think in terms of coincidence, he knew without question the two murders were related. Still, there was something missing—something important omitted from authorities' reports.

The logical thing would be to hop a flight for an up close and personal with Belle and Oliver Cunningham—flying, however, was out of the question. So, the obvious choice was a quick ring to the Yard to obtain contact information, and he'd find out what he needed to know in a phone call.

Within the hour, he listened as Oliver recounted his wife's discovery. "It was bloody disgusting—how an arm wound up on our garden terrace, I'll never know!" He paused, recalling the grisly scene. "And, that flower clutched in the hand? How did that happen?"

Santoro sat up a little straighter. "A flower?"

"Yes! In the middle of winter—a bloody calla lily!"

"The calla lily was bloody?"

Oliver paused, wondering if the chief inspector were serious. "No, no—there wasn't a speck of blood on it!"

Fifteen minutes into their conversation, Santoro finally rang off, a slight smile on his lips.

Finally.

A connection.

The second day of Paris Fashion Week underway, few gave thought to those who were no longer with them. Madelinne's name cropped up among friends until they no longer kept her in the forefront of their minds, and Chiara's memory was banked to a compartment rarely considered.

Compared to their first show in New York, Colbie and Kevin barely made an appearance, and there was little doubt no one noticed.

Except Luca Russo.

Colbie's presence at the runway shows was of little importance mainly because she knew nothing about the industry—it was what she did know that made him think twice. He found her absence curious, making him speculate she was investigating something that may involve him. A guilty conscious? Perhaps. More likely?

Arrogance.

Thirty minutes later, he opened the coffee shop's door, his eye catching Oscar's the moment he crossed the threshold. As Russo approached, Hallberg's body language provided no clue as to the designer's mood. "Oscar—how delightful to see you!"

Obligatory handshakes out of the way, both sat, scanning the small room—clearly, Oscar Hallberg had something private to discuss. *But, if that's the case,* Luca considered, *why not meet at his hotel?* When he thought about it, though, it made sense—Oscar loved being seen, so when an opportunity presented itself, especially among the peasants, who was he not to take advantage?

Hallberg ordered for both, the counter gal bringing their coffee soon after they sat down. "So—I can well imagine you're wondering why I asked to see you, Luca . . ."

"Yes—although, I haven't given it too much thought since your note arrived." He paused, watching the man across from him test his coffee for a suitable temp. "I can only assume it's important . . ."

"It is . . ." A pause. "It's come to my attention, Luca, you may no longer be happy in your present employment situation . . ."

Russo's eyebrows arched. "Unhappy?"

"Yes—I'm sure you know there's talk."

"About . . ."

"You. Armond. Your duties . . ."

Luca swallowed hard, then took a sip, followed by pouring in a little more cream. "I'm not certain of your source, Oscar, but nothing could be further from the truth." A slow sip. "You know I've been with Armond for decades— it's foolish to think I'd jump ship now."

"Jump ship? An interesting choice of words . . ."

"You know what I mean—besides, what would Armond do without me?"

"Well—I've known Armond Coniglio for many years, and I'm certain he would fill your shoes with a single phone call."

Russo was quiet, Hallberg's truth hitting home. "My situation with Armond is none of your concern—so, why don't you tell me why I'm here."

"The truth? I wanted to see if it were true . . ."

"You could have called . . ."

"Yes—but, I wouldn't have been able to see your face, would I?" He hesitated, shooting Luca an odd look. "And, your face, Luca, tells me you're lying . . ."

Luca felt a flush, then spontaneous heat traveling up neck.

"Please—you don't have to confirm, or deny. I already know the answer . . ."

Russo stood, his face more crimson by the second. "There is nothing to confirm—or, deny. Now, if you'll excuse me . . ."

Oscar Hallberg stayed seated, looking up into Luca's eyes. "I mean no disrespect. So, I will end our meeting with this . . . there are options, Luca. When you think about it, you know Armond Coniglio is a ruthless man—if he no longer requires your devotion, jeopardy follows."

Luca said nothing, listening to every word.

"So, should you wish to change your circumstances . . ."

"So, what happened when you met with Kara Vaughn?" Ryan grabbed a bottle of water from the fridge, then joined Colbie on the couch.

"Geez—I can't believe that was yesterday!"

"I know—neither of us have any free time, including Kevin."

"Have you heard from him today?"

"Briefly—he was shooting a couple of the runway shows just to keep up appearances. Then, I think he said he was going to dredge up more information on Hallberg . . ."

Colbie put on her glasses, then opened her laptop. "I don't know—his involvement in any of this seems a stretch."

"You're the one who encouraged him . . ."

"I didn't exactly encourage him—but, I'm glad he's taking the initiative to check out every lead. Even if it's only a suspicion . . ." She thought for a second. "Okay—I encouraged him. But, I think he has pretty good intuition— so, if he says he has a feeling about something, I want to hear it."

Ryan groaned. "Oh, no! Two of you?"

Just as Colbie was about to answer, Kevin rapped on her door, eager to join the party. "You're never going to believe what I found out . . ." He, too, grabbed a water from the fridge, then made himself comfortable.

"About what?"

"Not what—who!"

Colbie glanced at Ryan, grinning. "He's like a little kid at Christmas!"

Ryan agreed, then focused on Kevin. "I take it this is about Hallberg . . ."

Kevin nodded, then fired up his laptop. "When I didn't find anything on the surface, I thought I'd do a little deep dive . . ."

"What do you mean?"

"You know—into parts of the web you don't want to get to know."

"Okay—give it to us. What did you find out?"

"Oscar Hallberg, Armond Coniglio, and Basile Duchon—were in business together at the beginning of their careers."

"What does that have to do with our case," Colbie asked.

"I knew you'd ask that—well, it so happens everything was hunky dory for the first couple of years, then their relationship dumped it."

"Why?"

"It seems there was a falling out between Hallberg and Coniglio . . ."

"What about Duchon?"

"Not so much—during those years his designs were always on the fringe of success."

"If that's the case, why were the other two in business with him?" Ryan stopped typing and squinted at the laptop screen, backspaced a couple of times, then returned his focus to Kevin. "Ready . . ."

"Who knows—but, it was no secret the difference between Hallberg and Coniglio was enough to disband their company, each preferring to go their separate ways."

Colbie waited until Ryan was caught up before asking her next question. "Do you have any idea of what it was about?"

Kevin smiled, knowing she was going to love what he had to reveal. "It had to do with fabrics . . ."

Colbie's eyebrows arched. "What?"

"You heard it right—although there was little on the public web, I located fabric companies on the dark web no one's ever heard of . . ."

Ryan wasn't quite sure he was buying it. "Wait—you mean fabrics are important enough to have a spot on the dark net?"

Kevin nodded. "Apparently so—it was a down and dirty fight before Hallberg decided to walk away. According to what I learned, he figured Coniglio would eventually pay the price for his actions . . ."

"Which were?"

"Fraud."

Colbie glanced at Ryan. "What does fabric have to do with fraud?" As strange as the concept was, she had no doubt the information Kevin dug up was the root of their investigation—it was no coincidence Kara Vaughan was involved, if only for her knowledge and experience.

"I'm not sure—I didn't get that far in my research. But, it seems to me the only thing it could be is saying a certain fabric is something, and it turns out that's not the case . . ."

The following silence said it all.

CHAPTER

21

*L*uca Russo sat opposite of Armond, curious why he was summoned at such a late hour. Although he was used to his boss's quirks, they were beginning to get on his nerves. *Maybe Hallberg is right*, he thought as Armond glared at him.

"I'm sure you know, Luca—how long have you been with me," Coniglio finally asked.

"Thirty-two years—if you count when I was young and stupid."

"Interesting . . . has anything changed?"

The not-so-veiled insult was well-targeted and, in that moment, Luca Russo knew why he was there—but, he'd be damned if he would allow it to happen on anything other than his terms. "Before you continue," he commented as he stood, "there is something you should know."

Coniglio said nothing.

"It is clear we will be parting ways as of this evening—a decision I support." Russo paused, not taking his eyes from Armond's. "But, I encourage you to consider our past relationship, Armond—the secrets we hold. The actions you condoned." Another pause. "I'm certain both of us have confidences we prefer remain unbroken . . ."

"Luca . . . your ignorance surprises me! Just because our business relationship has run its course is no reason to think I would betray you in any manner . . ."

Russo watched him carefully, waiting for Armond's always-proven tell of lying—seconds later, as Coniglio gently stroked the flower in his lapel, Luca had his answer. "I will leave you with this, Armond—I shall keep your confidences as I expect you will keep mine. It's safer that way . . ."

As Luca Russo headed for the suite's main entrance, he felt Coniglio's eyes follow every move. There would be no agreement between them for Coniglio was arrogant enough to think he was in charge. An erroneous assumption to be sure, but one that would work beautifully with Russo's next move in what was quickly turning into a classic game of chess—capture the king.

Do that, and everybody wins.

Watching videos of the London and Milan fashion shows was the last thing he felt like doing—most of the clothes looked weird to him, and he couldn't understand who would wear such things. No surprise—as a child, Santoro was a country boy with little appreciation for the finer things and, from the time he was five, what rang his bell was figuring out all the pieces to a puzzle.

Clearly nothing changed.

He sat back, keeping his eyes locked on the computer screen as models and designers strutted their stuff. Unsure of what he was looking for made things a little more difficult, but, when he saw it?

He'd know it.

And, that's exactly what happened when Armond Coniglio appeared within the camera's lens, his eyes darting from side to side to see who was watching. Santoro assumed it was because of his arrogance. *But,* he thought as he watched, *who's to say he wasn't watching his back?*

Then, as Coniglio stood unknowingly in front of what would come back to bite him in the ass, Santoro spotted it.

The calla lily.

"Being the superb partner and investigator I am," Ryan commented. "I decided to spend a little time reading reviews of the fashion shows . . ."

"I see—does that make you a superb partner, and investigator? I'm not so sure . . ." Colbie tried not to smile, enjoying the feeling of past investigations—when she and Ryan knew the rules of their relationship, and both refused to cross boundaries. Comfortable in their friendship, she knew she could always count on him—whether inside or outside of an investigation.

"Very funny—and, you're damned right it does!"

Colbie's eyes didn't leave her laptop screen until, finally, her smile won. "All of them? New York, London, and Milan?"

"Yep—it was interesting. It seems there was a dust up between Duchon and Armond—of which, I might point out, we knew nothing."

Finally, he had Colbie's complete attention. "What kind of dust up?"

"From what I understand, Coniglio was shooting his mouth off about Duchon's collection—'uninspired, and pedestrian,' I believe he said."

"That doesn't make sense—unless it were for publicity purposes only."

Ryan shook his head. "I don't think so—there's always a thread of truth. At first, I didn't think too much of it—until I recalled what Kevin uncovered about Duchon, Hallberg, and Coniglio being in business together."

Colbie was quiet, thinking of possible links between Coniglio's recent comments about Duchon's collection, and their burgeoning business relationship decades prior. "Maybe all wasn't forgiven . . ."

"Maybe. At any rate, I think it's worth looking at—there was something about the way Coniglio looked when he was being interviewed that reminded me of a mad dog. You know—you never want to look one in the eye."

"Are you saying he's mentally compromised?"

"Yep—well, I don't know for sure, but it's a feeling I got when watching the interview. He just came across as someone who's ready to blow . . ."

"Don't forget, though—the whole thing starting the feud between Duchon and Coniglio eons ago was because of fabric." Ryan paused. "And, I gotta say I still don't see how that can be a target for fraud . . . designs, yes. Fabric? No."

"I admit, I'm not sure either—but, one thing I am sure of is I need to have another conversation with Kara Vaughan."

"About?"

"What Basile Duchon has on Armond Coniglio . . ."

"It's time . . ." Luca Russo nearly whispered his words, well aware his life was about to change.

"Excellent! We must move quickly—we have little time, and it's imperative we meet tomorrow—early."

Moments later, they rang off, each knowing their actions would be heralded by many, and opposed by few—unfortunately, it was those few worrying him.

With a place and time in his mental calendar, he was off to do a little rudimentary surveillance—something a neophyte investigator would do.

Tail Armond Coniglio.

Chief Inspector Santoro appeared slightly blue as he disembarked his flight. Flying never agreed with him, and from the time he was a young adult, he vowed never to set heels on the floor of a plane.

Ever.

But, things change.

His last time in Paris was on a case twenty years prior and, if he had his choice, he'd never return. Even so, with the image of Armond Coniglio and the calla lily etched in his brain, he knew he was about to break Chiara's and Madelinne's murders wide open. Doing so was a thrill that never got old, its allure all-encompassing.

He checked his watch. His appointment with Paris's investigators as well as the Chief Inspector from London was at one o'clock—just enough time to park his bags at the hotel, and do a little recon for a one-man surveillance.

I'll tail him after the fashion show, he thought as he finally headed for police headquarters shortly after twelve-thirty. After all, there was no point in surveilling him when he was at the fashion show venue—besides, local authorities immediately put undercovers in place as soon as they learned of the reason for Santoro's visit.

The good thing about Kara Vaughan's position with Basile Duchon was she wasn't an integral part of the fashion shows—so, snagging another meeting with her midafternoon proved fairly easy. With such little time left before the close of the Paris Fashion Week, it was imperative Colbie dig for the truth with everyone within her circle of suspects. Unfortunately, that was the thing—there wasn't a circle of suspects.

After her last conversation with Ryan and, for the first time in her life, she entertained the idea of taking down her investigator shingle at the conclusion of their case. Numerous times during their current investigation she felt as if she didn't have a handle on things, and there was no figuring out why. She didn't bring it up with Ryan or Kevin, of course, but, as she walked the few blocks to a neighborhood bistro to meet Kara, she weighed in on her true thoughts— those not tainted by someone who'd known her for years, or a young, greenhorn investigator.

Since Brian's passing, there was no question something was missing in her life—nothing she could put her finger on, but it was enough to prompt her to reassess. She no longer felt the joy of what she was doing and, if she were to be completely honest with herself, she wasn't sure she would again.

Convinced her intuitive abilities were waning, Colbie felt as if she no longer had anything special to bring her clients other than years of experience—which certainly accounted for something. Still, she was known for her alternative approach to cases, and it was a crapshoot whether she'd still be in demand. For the first time in her life, the word 'retirement' crept into her vocabulary . . .

And, it scared the crap out of her.

As a man used to carrying out the most unpleasant of tasks, Luca Russo rarely had a tough time sleeping. The previous night?

Not a wink.

Armond Coniglio saturated his thoughts—if there were a shred of gossip about his contacting Oscar Hallberg, his life would certainly be over, and it would take Coniglio a grand total of five minutes to take action. *There's no question my replacement is someone used to making things happen, no matter the situation . . .*

He pulled on his French cuffs as he admired his reflection in the foyer mirror, making certain the custom-designed cuff links were doing their job. Recalling the previous day, he realized terminating his affiliation with Armond Coniglio was enormously satisfying—although, he would never understand it was Russo's decision to break professional ties, not his. Speculation would be rampant, of course, when news of what would be perceived as a mutual decision made the rounds. There were those in the 'everything Coniglio camp' who would rally around him no matter what—they, too, proving their arrogance and ignorance simply by association.

Luca straightened his tie, his thoughts turning to Hallberg, and their upcoming meeting. There was an edge in Oscar's voice he hadn't heard before, prompting him to remain vigilant. He was, after all, walking into what he considered a room of secrets—things of which he knew nothing.

Moments later, he smoothed his hair, then grabbed his black, woolen, duster-length coat.

Ready.

CHAPTER

22

Oscar Hallberg slid thumb drives across the table. "These have all the information you need," he commented, "including a layout of the venue."

"I'm not sure why we need it," Marguerite noted as she slid the drive into her bag. "All of us have been there more than once . . ."

"That may be—but, renovations in areas you never see are critical to our plan." He paused, taking time to look at each of them. "Do not deviate . . ."

At that moment, there was a rap on the door and, as usual, Giorgia was charged with greeting guests. "Are you expecting someone, Oscar?" She eyed him, knowing he was capable of the unexpected.

"Indeed—please, Giorgia, be gracious . . ."

"As if you have to remind me," she teased as she headed for the door. Moments later, a gasp, as well as an attempt to hide her surprise. "Luca!" Giorgia stepped aside as the invitation to enter. "This is quite a surprise . . ."

"I imagine it is . . ." He slipped off his coat, handing it to her. Then, approaching Oscar, he extended his hand, clearly surprised Marguerite Villanova was a guest, as well.

"I'm glad you decided to join us," Hallberg greeted, gesturing for Luca to take a seat. "I apologize for the quick notice of our meeting, but I'm sure you'll understand . . ."

"I hope so . . ."

"You and I have known each other for a long time, Luca," Giorgia commented as she took her seat. "Our conversations have been many over the years—talks requiring trust and, at times, secrecy." She eyed him, her voice businesslike. "I convinced Oscar you would be perfect for our plan . . ."

"And, what plan is that, Giorgia?"

A momentary silence. "Our plan to take out Armond Coniglio . . ."

Russo said nothing, allowing her words to settle.

"Surely," Oscar interjected, "you must be fed up with Armond's arrogance—and, you must also be aware of his faltering mental state."

"Mental state?"

"Oh, come on, Luca—surely, you've seen it! He's no longer a man to be trusted . . ."

"He's not the man you knew only five years ago," Marguerite offered. "It's clear he no longer thinks in terms of design—only power."

"And, domination . . ." Oscar sighed, the weight of their plan plaguing his thoughts.

"Kara Vaughan is also with us," Giorgia informed him, "but she's having a meeting with Colbie Colleen as we speak."

Russo listened, quickly assessing the situation. "What does Colbie Colleen have to do with you?"

"Nothing, really—except Basile Duchon hired her to infiltrate Armond's empire. That makes her interesting . . ."

"Infiltrate it for . . ."

"Evidence of fraud, Luca . . ." Hallberg paused, evaluating the man sitting across from him. There was no way to tell if Russo's dissatisfaction with his former employer were enough to tell them what they needed to know. "I'm certain you recall—years ago—when Armond, Basile, and I were in business together . . ."

Luca nodded. "Indeed . . ."

"It was then," Oscar continued, "I realized Armond Coniglio's true intent—and, it had nothing to do with fashion design."

"Then, what?"

"Power, and money—and, he did anything he could to get it, including throwing his business partners under the bus . . ." Hallberg paused, taking a sip of water. "I was young and stupid enough not to take it personally and, after licking my wounds, I realized the dissolution of our partnership was a necessity." Another pause. "Not so with Basile . . ."

"It was a grudge never to die," Giorgia added, her eyes locked on Russo.

Hallberg nodded. "That's why he hired an investigator—he desperately wants to even the playing field."

"But, how?" Luca glanced at all of them. "You've seen him—he's hardly the picture of a man capable of retribution."

"On that we agree . . ."

Luca was quiet for a moment. A man of questionable distinction, he certainly had little room to talk when it came to his part in nefarious situations. The current conversation, however?

A taste in his mouth he found repugnant.

He stood, cuing Giorgia it was time to fetch his coat. "What Armond Coniglio did or does no longer holds interest for me—whatever you're discussing is something in which I cannot be involved."

Oscar Hallberg took another sip of water. "You surprise me, Luca—I would have pegged you for much more of a man."

"Well, Oscar . . ." A pause. "I can only hope I'm not your greatest disappointment."

With that, he took his coat, headed for the door, then turned to address each of them. "What is it the Americans say?" He paused. "Ah, yes—'thin ice.'"

Marguerite, and Giorgia watched as the door closed behind him.

"Now what?" Giorgia asked.

Hallberg drained his glass. "Plan B . . ."

Chief Inspector Santoro said nothing as two members of the French Police Force reviewed his information. There was little doubt they would be compelled to act—his preliminary investigation laid the groundwork perfectly.

So he thought.

"We need more," the seasoned Paris homicide detective commented as he flipped through several photos of Armond Coniglio, Chiara Ricci, and Madelinne Gastineau.

"More? How much more do you need? Two young women are dead, both with a calla lily in their hands . . ."

"Still . . ."

"And, who do you know who wears such a flower?" He didn't extend the courtesy of waiting for their answer. "Armond Coniglio . . ." He paused, then lowered his voice purely for effect. "You know as well as I—Armond Coniglio is at the root of murdering those two women, even if he didn't pull the trigger . . ."

"We have operatives in place . . ."

"Let's hope they're enough . . ."

"I think it's time I hear everything," Colbie began, her tone tinged with impatience.

"I agree . . ."

"Then, why don't you tell me what Basile Duchon has on Armond Coniglio—besides Armond's throwing him under the bus years ago."

"You know about that?"

"Of course—but, that still doesn't tell me the real reason Basile hired me. Or, for that matter, what you have to do with it . . ."

Tears welled in Kara's eyes, quickly spilling onto her cheeks. "I didn't want any part of it . . ."

It was then Colbie realized Kara was a pawn in an elaborate scheme, much as she, Ryan, and Kevin were. "I see that," her voice becoming soft. Coaxing. "Honestly, Kara? I don't think you have the guts for what they're planning . . ."

"You know?"

"About the plan? Surely, you can't think I don't . . ."

A well-intentioned lie.

"How did you . . ."

Colbie shook her head. "That doesn't matter. What I need now is everything you know . . ."

Kara's shoulder's slumped, her resolve to be strong fading rapidly. "Okay . . ."

So, there they sat—two women surreptitiously involved in a sordid scheme, but only by the hands of others. By the time they stood on the sidewalk outside the bistro door, Kara Vaughan, Colbie was certain, was no longer a part of the fashion industry. She had enough and, after spilling her guts about Basile Duchon and Armond Coniglio, she figured it was time to get out while the gettin' was good.

As Colbie headed back to her hotel, she couldn't shake the feeling things were coming to a head. With only one day left of the Paris show, she had to rely on what she knew best.

Intuition.

Basile leaned back in his chair, closing his eyes, thoughts turning to what he had yet to accomplish. If everything went according to plan, his glory would be great. If not? Well, it really didn't matter—he would gain personal gratification because he did everything possible to correct an egregious injustice.

He expected a few hiccups—what he didn't expect, however, was Kara Vaughan's tendering her resignation, effective immediately. Without going into detail, she briefly explained in a text she no longer had a hunger for the fashion industry, and she was leaving it altogether. That was it—no explanation and, from her final words, she was probably already on a flight to the States. *You matter not to me*, he thought as he deleted her text.

"Are you comfortable?" A nurse checked his pulse, then fiddled with his I.V. "You have about an hour to go . . ."

He smiled, appreciating her attentiveness. "I'm fine . . ."

But, Basile Duchon wasn't fine.

A closely-held illness was staking its final claim. The raw fact? Time was running out. In his mind, taking care of business with Armond Coniglio was a now or never thing.

There would be no second chance.

After ordering room service, Colbie, Ryan, and Kevin settled in for a final briefing before the last day of the Paris show. "Let's start with your meeting with Kara," Ryan suggested as he opened his laptop.

Colbie nodded. "She's gone . . ."

Kevin glanced at Ryan, then focused again on his partner. "What do you mean she's gone?"

"It was weird—after she told me about the fabric connection, she said she was done. She lost her taste for the design industry . . ."

"So she just . . . left?"

"I think so—right before we parted ways, she said she was going to message Basile to let him know she was out." Colbie paused, thinking about the gentle, middle-aged blonde. "I think she realized she was in way over her head, and she didn't want any part of it. At least, that's what she said . . ."

"A part of what?"

Colbie eyed both of them. "Get ready . . ." She paused, waiting for them to get comfortable. "Okay—it goes back to the days when Hallberg, Coniglio, and Duchon were in business together. It didn't take long for bad blood to develop between Armond and Basile and, as we suspected, Hallberg stayed in the background, refusing to get involved."

"Smart move . . ." Ryan typed a few notes, then turned to Kevin. "We wouldn't have known anything about that, if it weren't for you . . ."

Kevin grinned, enjoying the compliment. "Thanks—but, what was the whole thing about?"

"Fabric—Basile discovered a luxury fabric similar to silk, and Armond wanted it."

"How did Armond know about it?"

Colbie smiled. "Kara Vaughan's sister—when we met at the bistro, Kara told me her sister is the one who got her into the business in the first place. And, who was Kara to argue? The life was exciting, she was a young master at creating and sourcing fabrics, and it was a chance to travel the world . . ."

"So—how did her sister know about the fabric feud?"

"Because she worked for Armond Coniglio—and, that's how Kara got her position with him several years later when her sister decided to call it a day, and raise a family."

Ryan typed a few notes. "Okay—so what happened?"

"Armond Coniglio wasn't going to be denied—he paid big bucks to have someone create a fabric identical to Basile's."

"What?"

"Yep—and, Armond's time to walk the runway was before Basile's."

Kevin's eyebrows arched, realizing where Colbie was going. "Stealing Duchon's thunder . . ."

"Exactly . . ."

"Wait . . ." Ryan typed quickly, then focused on Colbie. "What about Duchon? If their fabrics were identical, how could he show his collection, and not be ridiculed?"

"Or, accused of some sort of theft—or, fraud." Kevin thought for a moment. "Something like that at an upscale runway show? It could've ruined Duchon for life . . ."

Colbie agreed. "It nearly did—that's when he went underground, fearful if he remained in the public eye, Armond was capable of doing it again . . ."

"He was probably right . . ."

Each was quiet, thinking about how things went down. "Is that why Basile hired us? Does he think Armond is going to do the same thing at this show," Ryan finally asked.

"According to Kara Vaughan, yes . . ."

Ryan shook his head. "I don't know—it sounds like a fear of someone slightly off his rocker . . ."

"I know—and, I think your observation isn't far from the truth."

Kevin was quiet, his silence charged with simmering anger. "Two people died—and, for what? Fabric? Fame? A screwy sense of injustice?"

Colbie tucked her legs beneath her, then took a sip of her favorite tea. "That's the thing, isn't it? Chiara Ricci and Madelinne Gastineau paid the ultimate price for greed . . ."

Again, they were silent. "There's still something missing—what about Hallberg?"

"Here's where it gets really interesting—Hallberg may have been flying under the radar way back when, but he never forgot what Coniglio did to Basile. It was then he vowed to take Armond down—but, he needed help to do it."

"Who?"

"Giorgia Mancini, Marguerite Villanova, and Kara Vaughn . . ."

"What?"

"Yep—because of Kara's uncanny ability to create and source fabrics, she knew where to go, and who to contact to recreate Armond's fabrics for tomorrow night's show."

"She did that?"

"Yes—although, she regrets her involvement now."

Kevin stood, and began pacing. "So, you're saying at tomorrow night's final runway, Basile Duchon is going to do the same thing to Coniglio that Armond did to him so many years ago . . ."

"Yep. According to Kara . . ."

"Holy shit . . ."

CHAPTER

23

The elevator's silence gave Luca Russo plenty of opportunity to think how best to present his information. Armond wasn't thrilled at the idea of being in his presence, but, when Luca advised he had information he needed to know . . .

Audience granted.

As the doors slid open, Armond's new man stood ready to lead him to the small sitting area within the massive suite. "He's expecting you," was his only comment. "Sit . . ."

A man with no class, Luca observed as the hulk stood beside him until Armond approached.

With a dismissive nod, Armond sat, waiting to speak until his new employee left the room. "So, Luca—I assume you have a good reason for contacting me."

In that moment, Luca wondered if he did the right thing. "I wouldn't presume to waste your time, Armond . . ."

"Then get to it—I must leave for the runway shortly."

Luca shifted his weight, eyeing his former boss. "I had an interesting meeting yesterday . . ."

Armond smoothed his tie, then adjusted the calla lily anchored on his lapel. "How can a meeting interest me?"

"Because the meeting was about you, Armond . . ."

That tidbit got his attention.

"Continue . . ."

"Although I have no particulars, it's clear there's a plan to discredit you . . . or, worse."

Coniglio looked stunned for a moment, then laughed, his voice raspy, and harsh. "Discredit me?" He thought about it, then appeared slightly amused. "Who can possibly discredit me?"

"Oscar Hallberg, Giorgia Mancini, and Marguerite Villanova to name three. Kara Vaughan, as well . . ."

Luca watched as a deep flush began to creep up Armond's neck, his face bright crimson within seconds. There was no doubt he would consider any action against him an unforgivable betrayal. "What do you know," he asked, his cigar-shaped fingers caressing the lily, then crushing it with a single squeeze.

"Only that—but, they asked of my interest to join them. An invitation I politely declined . . ."

Armond said nothing as Luca rose to leave. "I found their request distasteful—so, I left," Luca commented.

Coniglio glared at him, his eyes black with hate. "Perhaps I made the wrong decision by dismissing you . . ."

"It was I who chose to leave, Armond—there was no dismissing about it."

With that, Luca Russo strode toward the door, well aware if Armond Coniglio chose to do so, he could ruin his life. It was a situation he didn't enjoy, and the thought of living life elsewhere and out of the fashion industry was becoming more attractive . . .

And, a decided reality.

CHAPTER

24

*A*lthough few knew it, Oscar Hallberg was a man of tradition. Ritual. Superstition. Since childhood, he was of the mind if he didn't do things exactly the same way each time, misfortune would surely beset him—a chance he was unwilling to take.

Then, and now.

Of course, Luca Russo's refusal to join him in his quest to take Armond Coniglio down a peg or two was an unforeseen distraction—but, certainly not one important enough to cause derailing from his original plan. *Everything is in place,* he thought as he caught Basile's arrival at the runway venue from the corner of his eye.

He watched as the limo driver helped the designer from the car, his health in obvious question. Slowly, a young assistant at his side, they made their way to a private door complete with security, disappearing as a guard gently opened, then closed the door behind them. From there, Hallberg surmised, Duchon would take his place backstage, patiently waiting for his moment in the sun.

But, there was something about the way Basile looked, piquing his interest—something different about him. His pallor heightened more than usual, the manner in which he carried himself was an instant concern, causing Hallberg to question the designer's ability to walk the runway with his models.

Discreetly, he followed, greeting the guards as if they were old friends. Moments later—alone—he entered a darkened hallway leading into the depths of the event hall—a place where dark, wicked deeds could be carried out with little thought or concern of discovery.

In the distance, he heard Basile's voice, weakened to the point of a barely audible whisper. "You made arrangements," he asked the young man at his side.

"Yes—and, this is where I leave you. From this point on, Basile, you are on your own . . ." With that, the assistant mumbled a quick goodbye, then vanished into the bowels of runway construction.

Hallberg watched as the frail designer picked up what appeared to be a duffel bag, then climbed several, temporary, makeshift stairs to a small room, each step slow. Methodical. Tortured. Upon reaching the top, he stopped, chest heaving with each breath as he shifted the bag, opened the door, then stepped inside.

Silently, he closed the door.

As Oscar watched, he wondered—was there an opportunity before him which could take his plan to a new level? Perhaps—and, if there were, he would certainly make the most of it. Ask anyone who knew him—Oscar Hallberg could take any situation, and turn it into something to benefit him no matter the time, nor place.

He considered his ability clever.

Most thought otherwise.

He waited a few minutes, curious as to whether Duchon would emerge—when he didn't, the designer sensed the Fates working in his favor.

Threading his way through ground-floor scaffolding, he reached the stairs, considering his actions when reaching the top. Of course, he wasn't quite sure what he would find when opening the door, but, at the least, he could claim he was concerned about Duchon's health if things didn't go well.

Gently, he knocked, waiting for a response.

Nothing.

Another.

Again, nothing.

Scanning the area below for anyone who may be paying attention, he realized he was alone—except for Duchon.

Quietly, he turned the latch.

Before him, Basile Duchon sat in a folding chair, staring out a small window, watching the crowd gather for the main runway—to his right, an unzipped duffel bag.

"Basile?" Hallberg waited, then stepped forward.

"What is it you want, Oscar?"

"I was concerned . . ."

"About?"

"You, Basile—I saw you arrive, and it appears your health is more compromised than the last time we met."

"The time when you refused to help me?"

Hallberg swallowed hard, not caring for the edge in his colleague's voice. "It wasn't that I refused to help you . . ."

Without turning to extend the courtesy of looking Oscar in the eye, Basile Duchon's voice strengthened. "Then, what was it? You knew Armond succeeded in destroying my life, yet you refused to provide assistance in my effort to get it back . . ."

"I wasn't refusing you, Basile—your plan merely made no sense as far as my career was concerned."

It was then Hallberg spied the silenced rifle.

Set on its butt directly in front of Duchon, there was no question why it was there. His eyes following the targeted view, he suddenly realized the mission of a man completely destroyed by greed—but, not his own.

"Basile . . ."

"Leave me, Oscar. It is too late to change the course of things . . ."

In times of complete realization, it's often difficult to make the most prudent decisions. For Oscar?

Decision made.

In that moment, he recognized the truth of spontaneous opportunity—Basile Duchon would carry out what Hallberg planned, only in a different manner, and at a different time.

It was perfect, really—if he allowed the designer to perform an act that would, most certainly, end Armond Coniglio's stellar career, who was he to stop him? The fact was no one saw him follow Duchon into the runway's underbelly. As far as he surmised, there was no way he could be involved—and, from the look of him, Duchon's days were numbered, as well.

He smiled at the thought of no one's being left to refute what he knew to be true—Duchon had a score to settle. "I understand your pain, Basile . . ."

"You understand nothing! It is I who will take my last breath knowing I'm ridding humanity of an evil most do not understand! It is I who will take a stand!"

Hallberg said nothing, watching his once-partner's chest struggle to breathe. Then, with no more to be said, he stepped backward through the small door, closing it quietly.

There was nothing he could do.

Nothing he wanted to do.

CHAPTER

25

*C*olbie watched as main runway seats filled to capacity, celebs, starlets, and big names in the biz purposefully placed front and center, adding to the allure of the prestigious event.

"If I didn't know better," she commented to Kevin as they stood inconspicuously tucked into shadows, "I'd think those guys are cops . . ." She nodded toward a guy standing across the room from them, eyes trained on everyone taking a seat.

"Why would cops be here?"

"I have no idea—but, I'll bet my last dollar they're undercover. I feel it . . ."

Kevin grinned, again impressed by Colbie's abilities. "Well, if you're right, they're probably here as security . . ."

"Maybe . . ." She continued to watch, recognizing a glance to another undercover standing by the entrance of the runway. "There's the second one . . ."

Kevin glanced in the direction of the runway, then turned his attention to his cameras as if adjusting the lens. When planning their evening, they decided to continue their ruse as Valentine and her cameraman—after all, no one, other than a few key players knew of their true identities, and it provided Kevin an opportunity to take photographs should there be need.

"The final runway isn't until later," she commented, checking her watch.

"I'll tell ya—if I never see another runway, it will be too soon for me!"

"Agreed—I'm not sure I'll wear designer clothes again!" She laughed, but mostly for show.

From the time of their arrival, designers, models, and celebrities came and went, the venue emptying at the end of each. It was during those times Colbie and Kevin made their way backstage, paying particular attention to the models for top designers.

"There's Hallberg," she noted, scanning the room for anyone else who could keep her attention.

"I saw him—but, there's no sign of Duchon, or Armond." Kevin glanced at the clock on the backstage wall. "It's getting a little late . . ."

"Maybe—but, I suspect Armond Coniglio favors making an entrance. He and Basile are the last two collections to show . . ."

A quick turn backstage yielded little and, minutes before show time, they returned to their positions in the shadows.

"Who's first," Kevin asked, watching the house lights dim.

"Basile . . ."

Just as she answered, the runway illuminated as a model wearing Duchon's first piece in his collection appeared in silhouette. Then, walking its length and stopping at the end for camera shots as well as appreciative looks, she turned, allowing the stunning fabric to flow around her feet like gentle waves.

"Absolutely beautiful," Colbie murmured, admiring her client's talent for design.

As models took their turns, audience members smiled as they disappeared around the corner to backstage. Then?

Basile Duchon's final piece.

The audience gasped as the model appeared on the runway with nothing but silence and soft, glowing light to guide her way. No music. Nothing special.

Just silence.

The piece was ethereal.

The willowy model glided down the runway, fabric moving like gossamer wings. Colbie glanced at Kevin, then slightly past him, noticing Armond Coniglio standing almost out of sight. "Take pics—position, eleven o'clock."

Without obvious acknowledgment, Kevin turned his lens in that direction, nothing to indicate he was taking photos of those other than the audience. Colbie kept Armond in her peripheral vision, taking mental note—and, judging from the minute or two she had him in her sight, he wasn't happy.

As runway lights faded and house lights rose, Colbie scanned the audience, noticing the undercovers were no longer in position. "I have a bad feeling," she whispered.

Kevin didn't look at her, keeping his attention on his camera, and the audience. "Oh, great—what kind of feeling?"

"I'm not sure, but my radar . . ."

"About Armond?"

"Probably—the expression on his face when Duchon's last look walked the runway was one I wouldn't want to see often."

"Pissed?"

"Oh, yes—but, controlled. I saw him turn to his man and say something, then they were gone." Colbie paused. "Did you get pictures of him?"

"Yep . . ." Kevin finally looked at her. "Did you notice Duchon didn't walk with his last look model?"

"I did. Odd . . ."

"He walked the three last shows—why not this one?"

"I don't know—but, something's sure as hell different."

Basile sat quietly, thinking of Oscar, his breathing labored. Shallow. Quickly, he scanned the tiny room—the size of a closet, really—assessing everything was as it should be. Again, he arranged his chair so it was perfectly placed in front of the small window, allowing an unencumbered view of the runway.

Perfect, he thought as he made himself comfortable. *Très bien . . .*

"There is no time!" Armond Coniglio's face contorted with consuming rage. "Take it out! Take it out!"

Then, nothing.

The moment he realized the strength of his words, he also knew there was no question Basile Duchon was sending a message. *I will not be humiliated,* he screamed to himself as he headed for his backstage model line up. "You! You!" He grabbed the model's arm, wrenching it as he pulled her from the line. "You will not walk!"

Judging from the look on his face, the model decided it wasn't the best time to question his judgment. She did, however, jerk her arm from his grasp, well aware of his penchant for mistreating those in his employ.

Suddenly, the runway flooded with light, the first model in his collection beginning her walk.

Horrified, he watched as she stepped into his nightmare.

I must not give him the satisfaction, he thought, as each model took her turn. But, when the twelfth didn't show, heads turned, whispers snaking their way through the audience.

It was then, head held high, he took his rightful place behind the last model as the collection took its final spin. Applause was less than thunderous—tainted, of course, by the missing last look. But, though he was thinking of ways to effect well-deserved revenge, nonetheless, he reveled in the limelight, his place in fashion history preserved.

Approaching the end of the runway, he posed for photos, camera lights flashing. Suddenly, as the winter collection music reached its pinnacle, his knees buckled and he dropped, his face smashing onto the runway, eyes open, and staring.

Horrified gasps dwindled to petrified silence as Armond Coniglio lay on the stark runway, a hole in his forehead the size of a dime, the calla lily in his lapel stained with blood.

Undercovers leapt to action as Colbie and Kevin stayed obscured in the shadows, observing. "Any idea of where it came from," she whispered to Kevin.

"It had to come from up there . . ."

Colbie glanced at the small window near the top of the stage wall. "You're right . . ."

"What is that?"

"Probably the sound booth—or, something having to do with the production."

"It's really dark . . ."

"It would be, so that's not weird, But, based on the location of the bullet hole—smack dab in the middle of his forehead? It was a straight-on shot . . ."

Kevin nodded. "Let's check it out . . ."

With chaos for cover, they slipped from the venue unnoticed, eventually threading their way through posted construction scaffolding. "This is it," Colbie commented, looking to the top of temporary stairs.

"I'll go first," Kevin suggested as he started to climb, then stopped on the top step. "The door's ajar . . ."

"Can you see in?"

"Not really . . ."

"Let me see . . ."

Kevin moved to the side of the narrow steps, allowing Colbie enough room to sidle by. "Something's not right," she murmured as she carefully opened the door. There, slumped in a folding chair, was Basile Duchon, a silenced sniper rifle directly in front of him.

"Holy shit!"

Kevin tried to peer around her. "What?"

Colbie was quiet for a moment, feeling the sadness of such a tortured soul. "It's Basile . . ."

He knew from her voice, it wasn't good.

"He's dead . . ." She stepped aside. "Look . . ."

"Holy crap—he's skin and bones!"

Colbie snapped mental photos of her client's body. When authorities learned Kevin was a photographer, there was little doubt they'd request the digital card.

Other than the rifle, there was nothing in the room but minimal sound equipment, and the chair. "He had to have paid someone off—you know damned well a gig of this size has a regular sound guy."

"I know—that, however, probably wouldn't have been too hard to make happen. Everyone can be bought if it's for the right price—and, this isn't the main sound room."

They stood in reverent silence, each feeling it was what Basile deserved—until authorities spied them at the top of the stairs. Making their way down, Colbie knew she was in for a late evening of questioning, especially when they learned her identity.

She was right.

After describing the scene in the sound booth, she and Kevin were directed to wait until someone in charge elected to speak with them. Three hours later?

Free to go.

CHAPTER

25

After working closely with authorities to unravel events leading to Armond Coniglio's unexpected demise, Colbie, Ryan, and Kevin headed home to Geneva, each ready for time off.

"We're taking at least two weeks," Colbie ordered, as they parted ways at the airport. "I don't want to hear from either of you!"

Grinning and with a promise to obey, they separated, leaving Colbie to find her way home. Ryan learned years prior she preferred to keep to herself rather than go through the manners thing of seeing her to her door.

Within the hour, she stepped across the threshold to her apartment, enjoying the thought of spending time alone. It had been a long time since she had such an opportunity, and she could tell from her energy, she was in desperate need of a mental, physical, and spiritual reboot. *I can't wait to take a hot bath*, she thought as she kicked off her shoes into the closet.

Twenty minutes later, she eased into the tub, bubbles up to her chin. Closing her eyes, she allowed her body and mind to drift into meditation, providing the quiet solace she knew she needed—and, time to think about things she didn't want to admit.

But, must.

Within moments, her mind drifted into intuitive silence, events of the Fashion Week investigation at the forefront. Her eyelids fluttered as she watched images flash in and out of her mind, finally lingering for a moment or two on Luca Russo.

Since the conclusion of the case, he hadn't been seen or heard, especially in any of his go-to places for a bite to eat, or a midnight cocktail. *Actions,* Colbie considered, *of a man guilty of more than a poor choice of employers . . .*

Then, a fleeting image of an arm. A crushed calla lily. Madelinne Gastineau. In that moment, Colbie knew instantly they were linked by one man . . .

Russo.

During their investigation, she admitted to a brief moment when she considered him charming with a certain air of sophistication—something she appreciated, but only to a certain degree. If she had her choice, she'd always go for someone more down to earth. Grounded. A regular guy.

Like Brian.

Tears welled as she thought of him, hardly believing it was over two years since his passing. The months following proving difficult, she often considered backing out of the investigation business altogether—but, when Ryan suggested working together again, it seemed right. Something she should do.

Something Brian would want her to do.

And, that was the thing—it never seriously occurred to her she was growing weary of it until Armond Coniglio hit the dirt on the runway. The travel. Stress. Never having time to herself. While it was exciting in the beginning, within the last year she began to feel burdened, wondering if it were time to do something else.

Of course, she couldn't broach the subject with Ryan or Kevin, knowing it would do nothing but cause uncertainty in their lives. How could she? *They've been so good for me,* she thought as she turned on the hot water with her foot. Even so, she couldn't shake the feeling there was something else . . .

What, she had no idea.

True to their word, no one opened the office for a fortnight—Kevin flew home to see his family while Ryan decided on vacation time in the Caribbean.

"You look like Ernest Hemingway," Colbie laughed when he walked in the door, tanned and relaxed.

"Think so?" Ryan grabbed his customary bottle of water from the small fridge, then parked at his desk. "So—any news about the case?"

"Not really—but, it's no surprise. Authorities have their work cut out for them, but there's no doubt they'll pin Armond's murder on Duchon . . ."

"Agreed." He paused, thinking about the ancillary players. "The thing I wonder about is Hallberg, Giorgia, Marguerite, and Kara Vaughan—their scheme never really got off the ground. Duchon took matters into his own hands, don't you think?"

Colbie nodded. "But, we really don't know what their plan was . . ."

"I think it was to off Coniglio themselves . . ."

Again, Colbie agreed. "You may be right—at the very least, we know each of them will be hauled in for questioning."

For the next half hour, they discussed possibilities, finally deciding it was time to put the design industry in their case-closed file.

"So—what do we have on the books?" Ryan ran his fingers through his Hemingway hair. "I need a haircut . . ."

Colbie took off her glasses, leaning back in her chair. "Yes, you do . . ." She smiled, knowing what she had to say wouldn't be easy. "We had calls and a few emails requesting us to work on their cases, but I'm not sure . . ."

"Not sure? About . . ."

Colbie didn't say anything as she fiddled with a piece of paper on her desk.

Ryan took a gulp of water, then eyed her seriously. "That doesn't sound good . . ."

Finally she focused on him, still uncertain of what she would say. "Well . . . I've been thinking."

"Now it really doesn't sound good . . ." He paused, watching her carefully. It was a look he knew well—one telegraphing her need to talk about something. "Okay— what's up?"

"The thing is I'm not really sure . . ."

"About?"

"If I want to continue the investigation business . . ."

Ryan was quiet, allowing her words to rest in his brain—it was something he thought possible, but didn't expect. "Why?"

"Because I feel as if I'm losing myself . . ."

"I don't think I understand . . ."

"Well, you know what it was like when Brian was alive— we were always doing something."

"Okay—so, this is about your being lonely?"

Colbie shook her head. "No—not at all. It's more about I feel as if something is missing . . ."

"A relationship?"

"No—I feel as if I'm supposed to be doing something else."

"Like . . ."

"That's just it—I have no idea. But, I think I'm getting to the point where I want to find out what that is . . ."

Ryan placed his water bottle on the desk, then leaned forward in his chair, forearms resting on his knees. "What are you saying, Colbie? You want out of the partnership?"

"Well, not out—exactly. But, I think I need to take a sabbatical. You know . . . a leave of absence. After this case, I never felt as if we solved it—you know it was more like a series of events solved it. And, that makes me think it's time for a change . . ."

Ryan again fell silent, thinking. "I don't know how to help you," he finally commented, "but, I think you should follow your heart, and do whatever it is you think you have to do."

"If I do, what are your thoughts about keeping the partnership going with Kevin?"

"Well . . . I don't know. We work well together, so it doesn't really make sense to bag the whole thing now . . ." He paused. "If you leave, what are the chances of coming back?"

"Honestly, Ryan—I have no idea. All I know is *I think* it's time for me to move on . . ."

"Get out of investigations, altogether?"

"Maybe—one thing I know for certain is I'll move back to the States. As much as I like it here, I don't have the connection I have back in Seattle—or, anywhere else in the southern forty-eight, for that matter."

"It sounds as if your mind is made up . . ."

"Well . . . maybe it is. But, I still want to know what you think . . ."

Ryan pulled his chair closer to her desk, his attention solely on her. "I think, Colbie, you need to do what's right for you." A pause. "I know Brian's death was difficult for you—me, too. But—and, I have to be honest—you haven't been quite the same. Not that I expected you to be . . ."

Tears welled as Colbie thought back to the night she found out—the plane crash. News of no survivors. The crushing agony she felt when she realized she'd never see him again. "I know . . ." Her voice caught as she verbalized what she didn't want to admit.

"So," Ryan continued, "maybe it's time for you to haul in your shingle, and exchange it for something else. Maybe it's time . . ."

Eyes still shining with tears, Colbie looked at him, never appreciating his understanding more than she did at that moment. Her love for him would never end for he proved time and again the value of friendship. "I think it is," she admitted softly.

"I think it is . . ."

PROFESSIONAL ACKNOWLEDGMENTS

CHRYSALIS PUBLISHING AUTHOR SERVICES

L.A. O'NEIL, Editor
www.chrysalis-pub.com
chrysalispub@gmail.com

HIGH MOUNTAIN DESIGN

WYATT ILSLEY, Cover Design
www.highmountaindesign.com
hmdesign89@gmail.com